CornerStone

CornerStone

Rosewood

LAKEITH WOODS

authorHOUSE®

AuthorHouse™
1663 Liberty Drive
Bloomington, IN 47403
www.authorhouse.com
Phone: 1-800-839-8640

Published by AuthorHouse 03/23/2013

ISBN: 978-1-4817-2911-6 (sc)
ISBN: 978-1-4817-2910-9 (hc)
ISBN: 978-1-4817-2909-3 (e)

Library of Congress Control Number: 2013904606

DEDICATION

THIS BOOK IS DEDICATED TO MY

LIL BROTHER

IN MEMORY

ALEXANDER ANGELO BENNETT

(AKA) SMOKEY 1982-2000

YOU ARE A LOVED AND MISSED BROTHER.

MUCH LOVE AND RESPECT!

CONTENTS

CHAPTER ONE

The Beginning of the End

Rosewood:

Have you ever heard the saying what goes around comes around? Shit I didn't believe those words were so true, until dude I saw what come with them. I couldn't do nothing but be a playa about the situation, and take my hat of to them. I thought that I was the best at playing chess in the street, right now I may be in checkmate! I have been hit three times twice in the back and once in the elbow. Oh! By the way my name is Rosewoodd spelled with two d's as I say for a double dose of pimping.

Shit these cats go me hiding like I'm seven years old again; damn I am bleeding like a mother fucker! I never thought that four cats could get a playa like me pent down like this, even though I can't stand the police I wish they were here now. Shit they would charge me with burglary, since I did kick in this warehouse, dam I hear those cats.

One of the cats said. What's up Rose mother fucken wood? My job isn't done until I put two in your head. Rosewood.

At least let a playa die on his feet! Two of the cats picked me up and a third put his gun to my fore head and pulled the trigger, I heard a BANG! Then it happen . . . I saw my life flash before my eyes.

Rosewood Narrates:

That's me in the back seat of my father's 1965 continental with the kissing doors. My father was a player, the year is 1982 the place is St. Louis, MO. That's my mama on the passenger side she's pregnant with my little brother. The old dude was a mother fucker, I say that because of the shit that he use to do.

This nigga stayed clean like a white woman's kitchen floor in the 50's, and this nigga had ho's everywhere. What made him a playa was that my mama knew about all the ho's he had and she didn't care, as long as she spent time with him. When my old dude and I use to ride I use to see him in the streets making it happen. He would tell me about the game and the playas. He uses to tell me about respect and honor from the pimps, and hustlers. He also taught me how to watch out for the setup. As he use to say "The set up comes in lots of ways, you have con men, gold diggers, set up ho's, dope feens, and thousand of more games to the streets.

A playa gotta stay on top of all of the games and playas. He also has got to become a master of conversation; on the streets they call it selling a dream. The most important rule of all to the street life is dealing with killers and robbers in the game.

To be a true playa you must give them their respect, we call that a ghetto pass. At the time he was giving me the rules that I would end up living my life too many years later. As I said my father was a mother fucker, he had a bad side to him, he use to be on my mother if the wind blew to strong, shit I loved him I had to take the good with the bad.

I'm 14 years old, and today is a big day for my old dude, he has made his dream come true, He open his own club with his friend Jimmy. AI called him uncle JJ, he and my father go way back they came up selling tees and blues. Like I said before my pop had a mouth peace. The name of the club was the Apollo and I came there everyday after school. The club became a second home and it changed my life night by night.

I started to see the game in the raw, my father holding some of the biggest dice games in the city. As I went to school in the day learning the ways of the white people, I was so bored with the history of our country, I found myself falling in love with the schooling I had at night. Just think I was making more money at fourteen than some adults working good paying jobs. My mother and father always said to me that a man should always own his own! "There are two kind of people in the world those that work, and those that have you work". That has stayed with me throughout my life.

My name was popping in the streets I had respect from pimps, players, and hustlers. That's the cream of the crop on the streets white people call that life the underworld. At work at the club I found myself watching my father and uncle AJ all of the time, they were rolling with some big guys that had some real paper in the streets. One time a man from Detroit had his two boys in the club with him playing dice. They were about my age, when it was over these two niggas had about twenty thousand dollars! They broke them grown ass niggas! I was cheesing from ear to ear like I had put in some work The year was 1985 and the as I knew it, things would never be the same. This was the year crack hit the scene if you ask anyone in St. Louis, they would say in eighty seven that's when it hit the streets. The real playas started using and putting ho's on it in eighty five, when the so-called playa found out what was going on the game went south. That shit there took a lot of good playas out of the game it wasn't about the money anymore it was about the high. Brothers didn't have to be smooth anymore or clean, all he needed was the crack. One day after school I was working at the club, when I walked in on uncle J, it was cold outside and that nigga was sweating like he had stole something. The last few months Jimmy and my father had been having problems over money. My old dude was making it and Jimmy was smoking it up. My father's life was the club now we lived off the money from the club.

Jimmy was still in the streets so he was living of the fat of the land. When my little brother was born my old dude began to slow down, he stopped messing with ho's and low down dirty niggas. My mother use to tell him all the time if you lay down with dogs you get up with fleas. She didn't like Jimmy's ass at all, she always told my father that he was his down fall, and had many fights over that nigga,. As I look back on it Jimmy and my father came up from the streets together. My father kept growing and Jimmy was cool with the money from the streets. They were on two different levels in the game, my old dude tried to make Jimmy see the hold picture, but Jimmy was cool with the streets respecting his name. That wasn't enough anymore for my old dude, he wanted and needed white people to know and respect him and to know his name. It took me years to understand that one there.

I will never forget this day, I skipped school and went to the club. I went through the basement window so no one would know that I was there. I heard a group of men talking in the back room, uncle J was in charge I heard him saying "We have got to make some changes around here some of us think that they are better than the rest of us. The rest of the guys agreed with him. Then I heard one of the men say "What are we going to do about this problem? Jimmy said" I want say this out loud, you never know who is listening" So I will write it down, so pass it around and the last person give it back to me. About five minutes passed the room was real still. I heard one man say I ain't with that one! Jimmy got mad and said Mother fucker you work for me Bitch! I tell you what the fuck to do and when the fuck to do it! Do you understand? The man said, yes sir, Jimmy.

Jimmy then said you better understand mother fucker before I put your name on this paper. A few moments the room was silence, as I climbed down of the boxes of Hennessey that they stored in the basement of the club. I was confused about the conversation that I just over heard. I really wanted to know what was going on with uncle, Jimmy and the others. I wanted to know why my old dude wasn't there, the conversation sounded real important. It sounded like they were planning a capper. My mama always said that I was always curious my old dude said the boy is just nosey just like you. My mama said this like clock work "June fuck you nigga" he would laugh and smack her on her ass. Later on that night at home my old dude was locked in his study, he used to call it his war room. When he was in there you couldn't fuck with him it was about nine thirty at night. Knock. Knock. Knock, at the door was uncle, Jimmy. My mama told me to get my father. It felt like I was moving in slow motion, he was sitting at his desk with his head down counting that paper. For the first time I saw the safe open, he was smoking on a cigar and had a glass of crown royal on the desk. When he looked up he was real calm, that fucked me up, and usually when I came in like that he pitched a bitch and smacked me on the head, and would give me a speech on respect. This time he told me to come here, you see all this? I said yes sir, then he told me something that I will never forget, "A broke black man in this country has no voice in capitalist society. So if it don't make dollars it don't make sense!

Now what do you want? I said that Uncle Jimmy is in the front room. He asked me Rose did you understand what I told you. I said yes sir, Now tell Jimmy to give me a minute. I made my way back to the front room my mother was at the TV. With her back toward Uncle Jimmy, as he was sitting on the couch. I saw him looking at my mother like she was a piece of meat I guess he saw me out of the corner of his eye, he turned toward me and he told me to come here. Lil Rose what's up with my little playa. I said nothing Uncle Jimmy, he asked me why I didn't come by the club after school? I said that I had to cut this lady's grass up the street. He said that he had Little Jimmy at the club, he has a son but we don't see him that much. But I knew that the nigga was lying don't forget that I was in the basement skipping school today. My mother asked about lil Jimmy's mother, Ann he said you know that girl is crazy. My mama laugh and said she was crazy in high school, you said that's what you liked about her. He said shit I did didn't I.

Then my old dude hit the room, Jimmy said what's up June? My old dude said shit you tell me playboy. Then uncle, Jimmy pulled up on my old dude and whispered something in his ear. As I watched my old dudes face it was something that concerned him. His first step was toward the closet to grab his coat. When he did that my mother told him to come here, they walked to the bedroom, they were gone for about five minutes or less. That left me an uncle Jimmy in the front room alone. I asked Jimmy what was up He told me that they had to handle some business in the streets.

Then my old dude came back in the front room, and told Jimmy let's roll, My mother told my old dude that he shouldn't go she didn't feel good about that move. He said Ann I will be right back, as he walked out the door she yelled his name June! Don't go! I heard him say Ann I love you! I was now two o'clock in the morning and my mother had not went to sleep yet. As I laid in my room I could hear her walking through the house, from the kitchen to the front room. I could hear her open the blinds over and over again. Then the phone rang it must be the old dude. Then I heard her say the police, she said that June is not here and she hung up the phone. The police was always two steps behind, a lot of them dug my old dude Then the phone rang again, they said Ann, we know now where he is, we need you to come and identify the body, the man said June's body! I heard her scream and drop to her knees, and start crying.

I ran from my room and asked her what was wrong? She said over and over again, he's gone, he's gone, I asked her who's gone? She said June is dead! I just stood there looking crazy, I was so confused my mama was crying my old dude was dead and life stood at a stand still. My mother finally got herself together and took me over to my cousin's house on the north side of town. She didn't want me to go with her to see the old dude like that. On the way over to my cousin's house, my mother went from sad to mad. It messed me up the way she changed, she started thinking out loud, she said I told him not to go with that smoke ass nigga Jimmy! She said that over and over again.

We finally made it to my cousin's house, his mother started to ask questions. Ann what happen? Where did it happen? Who was with him? Did someone shoot him? What kind of shit was he in? My mother told Kim" Bitch stop asking me all of those god damn questions!! My man just got killed and you asking me all of those mother fucking questions! "Like you work for channel 4 news". She asked Kim are you going to watch Rose are not? Kim said girl you know I am. My mother ran out of the door all I heard was rubber when she left. My mouth was open when she left, I had never seen that side of my mama, I mean I never had seen it. Kim was still hot after my mama had left, she tried to play it off, but you could still see that shit face behind that fake ass smile. She told scrap and I to go to sleep. We went to his room scrap asked me what was going on? I told him what I knew, it wasn't much because my mama went off into here own world. My cousin scrap was cool people we were born a little under a year apart. When I use to spend the night over to his house we use to stay up all night talking about things like what's this? What's that? One thing I can say about the lil nigga was down for whatever, I mean whatever!

One time the nigga caught the bus over to my house from one side of town to the other, I know it doesn't sound like much but the nigga was only five and the first thing he said when he got off was Rose, I didn't have to pay!! The nigga was a rider for real. The only thing that I didn't like about spending the night was the only thing we would eat was hotdogs and pork n beans. But that nigga and I use to be all over the city on the bus for free.

Shit we lived at the zoo, movies, and skating rinks. I finally went to sleep when I woke up I heard my mama's voice in the kitchen talking to my cousin's mama Kim. I overheard her saying that my old dude got shot seven times. Five times to the chest, and two times point blank shots to the head. They say he was shot by a forty five hand gun, the police said that someone else was with him but they ran away from the scene. The police said that eight shots fired at the crime scene. Someone called the police when they heard the shots around nine forty five last night. So he was killed right after he left the crib. My mama told Kim, Girl I told him not to go, when I saw him I didn't see a face, I just knew that something wasn't right.

She got on the phone and called Detroit that is where my old dude was from, she was on the phone with my grandmother. She told her baby it's gonna be alright call me back in about a half an hour. See my old dude was a Detroit playa, niggas in St. Louis didn't really dig my old dude for real. Begin out of Detroit he had dope lines to New York, a Miami, Atlanta, Chi town, Dallas, Las Vegas, and all through Cali. My old dude had three brothers, and all of them had a spot in the game. They use to call it a trade in the game, so when he use to say that he was from a long line of players, pimps, and hustlers, it was true. He was taught to live of the fat of the land. Later on uncle Jimmy shows up and told my mama what happen. He told her that he believes he knows who did it. And not to worry about Nothing! I got you and lil Rose, I'll take care of you all.

My mama said, Jimmy you're strong as a mother fucker, how the fuck you got me, when June had you! Your best bet is to sell that dream to one of them dumb ho's you fuck with. Jimmy said Ann I know your mad! You damn right I'm mad I just lost my man the father of my son. I thought that you were his friend, Jimmy. He dropped his head and said I was. My mama said then why did you leave him? Why did it so long for you to come and see me? The police said, that it happened around nine forty five last night. Now it's six thirty pm the next day. Jimmy said, that he would come back when my mama cools off and then he left. After he left my mama said, I know that low down black bastard had a hand in June's death I can just feel it in my bones. She looked at me and asked if I was alright? I said mama I am confused she grabbed me and said, baby me too. The next day, I mean early the next morning there was a round of hard knocks at the door. BOOM! BOOM! BOOM! BOOM! BOOM! My mama jumped off the couch and ran to the door and asked who is it? It's me baby girl, who is me? Tarzan, open the door.

I looked out of the windows to see my real uncles from Detroit. Tarzan my old dude said was the king of the concert jungle. His trade in the game was robbery man and head knocker. Everyone in the game don't like them niggga's in that trade because no one was safe. My uncle Roosevelt he was the playboy of the group. AKA the pimp of the family, my old dude said, that nigga ain't had a real job since seventy two. All he did was talk shit and swallow spit, count doe and fuck ho's. He was also my God father, My old dude said that I move just like pimping Velt did when he was young.

That where I got my nick name lil Rose. They brought my baby uncle down here with them Pat. This nigga here was a dame fool, he was a mix of all of them nigga's, and he was my old dude cat. We moved from Detroit because my uncle Pat got locked up, and my old dude, knocked the fat meat out of the head of the only witness on the case. They had to let my uncle out and we moved to St. Louis. My mama had some people there. So here we are, we packed up something and got ready to go back to Detroit that's where the funeral is going to be held. My uncles were here to investigate and to security for my mother and me. They sat down and went through provide the last six months of my old dude's life. They wanted to know about all the people that he had fallen out with, they wanted to know about all the business he was doing and with who did he have any money tied up and who with? They wanted to know all about Jimmy, where did he work? How many kids did he have? Where does his mama live? How many people live there with her? What kind of drinks does he like? Did he do drugs what kind of drugs? Where is the club? Pat was in the corner with his head in his hands Pat asked my mama a question, Ann why did you move the fuck down here? My mama said Nigga! You know why the fuck we came down here now don't you! My uncles said, Pat shut the fuck up! Then they told my mama that they were going to claim the body. They would be back after they were done, get what she needed, because when they come back they would be on their way back to Detroit. I was sitting in front of the t v watching the a-team, I saw my mama in my old dudes study, when I walked in the safe was open, she looked at me and said if your daddy was here he would have a fit about us in his study. I said he would, I asked her how much money is that? she said, a little bit more than ninety thousand dollars. She told me not any one about this, I said Ok. My uncles came back and got my mother my lil brother and I, we all went to Detroit, When we got there my grandmother gave me a big hug and told me baby, everything is going to be alright and God will guide us through this, this too shall pass. There were so many people at the house most of them I had never seen before. My grandmother hit me on the butt and told me to go and play with my cousins. The last day I saw my old dude when they put him in the ground, it was raining and cold, the sky was dark grey. I saw strength in my mama and my grandmother on that sad day. They didn't drop a tear or there heads. They kept it gangsta as they lowered him in the ground. In my heart I knew he was smiling. That day I was forced to become a man.

CHAPTER TWO

Jimmy's Fifteen Minutes Of Fame

We stayed in Detroit for a month, my grandmother wanted to help my mother with my brother and me. The way I saw it was they where there for each other. Today was the day we were going back to St Louis. I guess we were going back to try to peace our life's back together again. It will never be the same with out my old dude. For the last month my mama has been telling her self that we will have to take life one day at a time, one day at a time.

We made it back to Lambert air port around two thirty in the morning. We caught a cab home. When we got there everything looked fine, until my mother turned on the lights! Someone had broken into our house, but they didn't take the T.V and things like that.

They busted holes all in the walls all over the house looking for some thing. When we walked in to my father's steady someone had took a blow torch to his safe and had cut off his door. My mom looked at me she didn't say anything, but I know what was going through her head. The only other person that knows about the safe is who? You take a guess? My mother called the police. It took them about five hours to come make a report. It felt like we had been up for a couple of day, because at big momma's house everyone gets up early. The plain ride was rough and now the police are asking my mother a lot of dumb ass questions. I heard the police say to my mother, I can see that they were looking for something. She looked him up and down and said, no shit Sherlock. Did you get your badge out of a lucky charms box! You fat bastard! I didn't help any I was on the floor rolling around laughing.

The police turned red in the face and asked my mother what was in the safe? My mother told him that when we moved in it was already in the wall. We always wanted to know what was in there. When it was all over they didn't find on prints or anything. They told us that it was a clean job. I heard my mama say bull shit! I guess you can see that my mother doesn't care for the law. We found our way back over Kim and Scrap house again.

We stayed over there for about two weeks. When my mother us to house hunt, scrap and I use to kick it. One day scrap and I went back to the club to see what was up with uncle Jimmy. It felt funny walking back in there knowing that my father wasn't there nor ever coming again. Everywhere I looked I saw him standing there. I told Scrap lets go and on the way out we ran into Uncle Jimmy coming in the door.

Jimmy looked at me and said, what's up lil rose I see you all are back in town. I came over to see if you all were all right, but you guys were gone. I came over a couple of more times but no one was there. Then he asked me how was my mother doing? I told him that she was ok I guess? Then he asked me where did we stay? Before I could say anything Scrap opened his big mouth and said, with us uncle Jimmy! He looked at Scrap and asked him was he Kim's boy? Scrap shook his head yeah. Jimmy smiled and reached in his pocket and gave him a couple dollars. He told me to come here. Then he told Scrap to go buy some candy or something lil playa. He looked around the room then he asked me did my mother have any money? I told him that my grandmother and uncles in Detroit gave her some money. He told me no lil man not money like that big money lil man big money! I told him no that I haven't seen anything like that. Then he walked towards the bar. He told the young chick behind the bar to poor him a drink. He turned back to me and said if I ever saw my father's safe open? I said yeah the one in the floor at the club. He stood up and said No boy! The one at your house in your father's steady. I said, oh I never seen that one open. Then I asked him a question. Did it open? I always thought it was broken. Then I said, Uncle Jimmy when we were out of town some one broke in our house and cut it out of the wall.

My mama told the police that it was there when we moved in. She said, that she always wanted to know what was in it. He laughed and gave me some money. Then he told me to come by after school and do my job and make some change. Then he told me that he was still my uncle. Then he asked me did my mother know that I was down here? I said, no. Then he told me not to tell her ok. Scrap and I jumped back on the bus headed home. I told Scrap not to say anything about us seeing Jimmy to my mother. He said, ok. Then I told him about Jimmy having something to do with my father's death. He looked at me crazy and said why didn't you tell me about that nigga earlier. I said damn I thought I did scrap. When we made it home I saw Jimmy's car out in front of the house. When we walked in Jimmy said, what's up lil playa's He was acting like he hasn't seen us to day. Then he looked at scrap and said, this must be lil scrap. Kim I haven't saw this boy since he was around two years old. Believe it or not Kim fell for that bullshit. Scrap and I looked at each other and walked to his room. Then scrap told me that Jimmy was a mother fucker. I set on his bed I said, one thing I can say about that nigga is that he has a mouth piece. Scrap shook his head and said, yes he does. Jimmy turned back towards my mother and Kim when we left the room. He was like Ann, what's up? My mother asked him why didn't he come to the wake He said, baby I know that the family needed time to get over there lost. By the way Detroit is a long way from home for me to be fucking with some Detroit nigga's right now.

My mother just looked at him and said, your ass didn't have a problem when yo ass was broke and couldn't rub two nickels together. You fuck with them Detroit nigga's then. He put his hand on her leg and said, baby girl that was then, this is now. It's all about the home team now baby girl. My mother stood up and said nigga what the fuck is up with all this baby girl shit. Jimmy stood up and said, that he has always loved that about her then he asked her if she needed some money? She said, no. All I need is the name of the nigga who did that to June. He said that he has been looking for him over a month now. My mother then asked him what was the guy's name that did that to June he asked her again if she needed any money. My mother dropped her head and said that she didn't need anything from your snack ass. Then she told him to get the fuck out of her house. When I saw that I come back in to the front room.

Jimmy jumped back up off the couch and said, bitch who the fuck do you think you talking to ho? I'll break your mother fucking neck bitch. I ain't your soft ass man. I'll make you touch ever thing in this mother. Bitch I was the muscle in the game that June and I played. I kept those nigga's off June's ass around this mother fucker. They would have sent his ass back to Detroit in a bag along time ago. When he got to the door he grabbed her hand and kissed it and said, bitch don't bite the hand that's trying to feed your stinking ass. Then he walked away cool as a mother fucker smiling. His driver opened his door for him. This nigga had a Cocaine white eighty six Fleetwood brougham lack. Don't forget it's nineteen eighty five. My mother didn't have anything to say. I mean at all.

As I stood at an angle behind my mother looking as Jimmy walked away. It was a sunny day, it seem like he was moving in slow motion. When Jimmy slid in the back seat and his driver closed the door The window was half way down. Jimmy looked at us one more time. He put on his shades and the window started to go up. At the same time my mother was closing the door. It seem like the door didn't close to his window was all the way up. Jimmy was on top he was a neighbor hood super star now. The cold thing about it was that he knew it. He was nigga rich, my father use to always tell me, getting the paper wasn't the hard part. Maintaining and growing it was the bitch. So when power comes. Comes struggle and with that comes envy. My father us to say with money and power will always show a man's true heart and attention towards his fellow man, and if I know Jimmy it's about to go the fuck down.

I feel for any one that get's in his way., because if it ain't about Jimmy, it about nothing, and you will pay one way or another. Jimmy use to say that the game was cold, but it's fair and then he would show that snack ass smile. Shit three months has passed. The street was talking Jimmy was pressing nigga's in the game. He had got a plug out of Denver. He was the first brother to tap off into Denver like that. Now Jimmy had the power and the hustle. Now he was putting the press on cats to become his muscle. Guys in St. Louis, was falling off one neighbor hood at a time. If they choose not to work for him They so call leader would end up in a rug in East St. Louis. Dead as a mother fucker.

That's a game that he knows well. He took the north side over in three months. His eyes were on the west side of town now. On the west side there was a nigga name Slick. He had the west on lock like a pawn shop in the middle of the project doing a race war. Jimmy sent some of his cat's over to the west to put the press game down. Those guys never came back to report in. these nigga's would bump heads at the playa's ball a month later. This year the playa's ball will be held in ST. Louis at the Adams Mark hotel. The Adams Mark was the most beautiful hotel in the city. Out front all you saw was limos and other high price cars. Three hundred and sixty five days of the years, it's only for people of power in the legit business world., but to night it would play host to some of the most powerful men in the under world game of big business. See the play's ball always attacked the whales of the games.

Playa's come from all over the bubbles to net work with each other. Most of them have heard of each other name if you are making any kind of noise in the game. Have you ever wonder how playa's made connection all over the bubble. Let' me take this time out to explain the word bubble. In the Webster's Dictionary the Europeans say, a small round object. In the game to a playa it means the world. In our case let's say the states. That was for the people who is kind of slow to the street life. Ok lets step back off in this shit we call the game. The playa's ball is a meeting place for pimps playa's, and hustle and the people that comes with that life. This is how they net work with each other. It's like the Grammy's they have in Holly Wood. They even have a red carpet and even give playa's an award that's at the top of there game. You even have a lot of people from the entertainment and the sports world. A lot of people don't know that a lot of sport stars and entertainment come from this life.

When you walked in the Adam Mark hotel the first thing you see is a doorman. Then you walk through the doors you see a big water fountain setting in the middle of the floor. It's trimmed in gold. The front desk sets off to the left side of the lobby. The carpet is a rose red and it has roses hand stitched in it.

The carpet matches the doorman, bell hops and front desk uniforms. Straight pass the fountain are two elevators from the ground floor to the top floor. You see it one of the world's most expensive Chandeliers in the states. At the same time you had playa's wearing fur coats, alligators shoes from city Slicker's out of Detroit. Ice the fuck out when you see them you know they are grown ass men. My uncle's were back in town for a couple of reason. One was to attend the playa's ball. And the other thing was that unfinished business. Jimmy and his crew were walking through the lobby. My uncle Tarzan was at the front desk when Jimmy walked passed him, my uncle Pat was standing by the ball room door shooting his mack at a chick,. my uncle Roosevelt was bringing up the rear on that nigga. He had three of his hoes riding dirty too, they had seven more guys in the ball room already on post. Then Slick and his crew walked in the lobby. Jimmy couldn't see my uncles because they were among the rest of the playa's. Slick saw Jimmy and yelled across the lobby. Jimmy turned around, Jimmy and Slick walked towards each other with there crew around them. As they stood toe to toe looking like boxers. Slick told Jimmy, nigga you was out of line sending your cat's in my neck of the woods.

With that lil boy games you re playing on the north side of town. Then Slick asked Jimmy, did they tell you what I said? Jimmy looked at him and said, No, I haven't seen them. Slick started laughing and stepped up on Jimmy. Now they are nose to nose. It was so quit you could hear a mother fucker heart beat. At the same time my uncle Tarzan gave Pat the sign to get the other cat's out of the ball room. Tarzan moved from the front desk, he is on the right side of Jimmy and Slick. Pat and the cat's are on the left side of Jimmy and Slick. Roosevelt and his ho's are at the door. Slick and Jimmy are still nose to nose. It was still quite on both side are picking someone to get down with. Then Slick says to Jimmy, Bitch ass nigga if you ever try some shit like that again. I'm going to send you, where they are at, ho ass nigga.

Soon as the word nigga came out of Slick mouth Pat saw the perfect opening to give Jimmy the blues. Pat started shooting from the left side of jimmy and the cats jump right in with no question asked. They were hitting everything in sight. Tarzan had to jump behind the water fountain that was the only thing that saved him that night. People were running around and dropping like flies. Roosevelt and his girl falls out the door and got behind some limo's out side. When pat and the cat's got finish shooting they all laid down on the ground. Then Tarzan saw Jimmy and a couple of his guys running for the door. He came from behind the water fountain. He had on a Full length black fur coat on with a fully automatic machine gun with a hundred round drum. I see why they call him Tarzan, when he stepped around that fountain with Jimmy in his sight. Tarzan gave him ever thing he had to offer. That mother fucker was spitting, and shells were every where. They use to have a glass entrance until Tarzan came to town and shot it out and Jimmy jumped through it. When he made it outside he stood alone.

My uncle Roosevelt went and got one car and one of his ho's got another When he pulled up the other girl was looking at Jimmy. I don't know how this nigga was still on his feet. They said that it was all the coke he was on. Jimmy was hit over twenty two times. The doctor said that the dope saved his life. Slick got hit in the face and three times in the back he lived too. Both of there crews got fuck around, the cold thing is that they think each other did this to them. They both went under ground to regroup. Now they are at war with each other. My uncles came over that night to get my mother, little brother, and I. To take us back to Detroit with them. My mother told me to go with my uncles and she would come later on. She had to handle some lose end to tied up. I was on my way to Detroit with no clothing or nothing. That was the last night I would see my mother or brother for a few years. Detroit was going to be my new home now. That night was a turning point for Jimmy in the game. Now he had to work on his crew a lot of them got killed that night at the Adams mark hotel. When he pulled up on cats and tried to sale them on why they should be on his team they wasn't biting. That night it was all over the bubble. The street was watching that night. The street was talking too. The news was moving from playa to playa like wild fire. The boys out of Denver pulled out there reason was that Jimmy had too much heat on him.

Then he was at war with Slick, when the boys from Denver use to drop work off every three weeks like clock work. That was the ball now it takes three to four months to move the same size packs. My father use to say that a business man must be willing to lose money when you are at war. You can't go to war when your money isn't right. See Jimmy wasn't ready for war. He was tricked off in to it, because in the street war you can't sale dope and nigga's shooting at you. Two things will always happen the police will always be on the set. When the police is on the set they will kill the set. Your customers you sale to don't fuck with the police they will go anywhere that has it. See Slick was smart he is at war with Jimmy on the north side of town. Slick was on the west side of town. They were both hitting each other at will. Slick west side hide out was a front. He moved everything to the south side of town. He also tied in with the boys from Denver they needed some one in the market. Slick was getting stronger and Jimmy was getting weaker the war was killing Jimmy him slowly. His connect pulled out on him and other cities knew he couldn't move the packs any more. So he was frozen out the game. He had to look for another hustle See the boys in Detroit had ties with the mob, on that work from the east coast to the west coast. There was a guy named Hen C he got the news that Jimmy was looking for some work out of ST Louis. Hen C was going to move some work that way. My uncle Tarzan heard the news and pulled up on Hen C. Tarzan told him about how Jimmy did my father. See Hen C and my father went way back. So Tarzan pick up the order Jimmy was trying to get a bird and a half of soft. So Tarzan put a stunner pack together. A stunner pack is a kilo of dope that is fake can be flour, baking soda and sugar. Put the zip of real in the middle of the pack. Tarzan liked to use real cocaine when you tap the middle it will be all good.

Tarzan put his cats in place they were the so call dealers to Jimmy. They met in chi town everything went through like clock work. Jimmy got his so called work, my uncle made fifty thousand dollars. Sees jimmy would find out it was fake. When he did it killed him that was his last life line. Tarzan the king of the jungle played him like the bitch that he was. Slick was fed up with the war between him and Jimmy. Slick had nigga's out side of the Apollo in a truck for two days. Jimmy pulled up in the front of his club with his crew. Slick boys wanted to wait until they went in. Then when they did they sat the back of the club on fire. When every one ran out of the front Slick boys was picking them apart one by one. Jimmy went through the trap door my father had put in and it saved that nigga life again. the rest of his crew was dead and Jimmy went back under ground and never been seen again. My father always made me practice my chess game, because he said, that you will have to out think your appointed on every level of the game. Jimmy use to just press he never took the time to put protection on his king you can't press with your king to. If you do there is no one to watch your back.

CHAPTER THREE

Lil Rose Starts To Bud

As we hit the highway, I'm riding with my uncle Roosevelt in his eighty six Cadillac. It's triple black with gold trimming, it has a gold CC grill on the front of it with the flying lady, on fifties and vogue tires. I was in the back between two of uncle Roosevelt women, it was about midnight it was quite in the. My uncle was playing I'm the pusher man by Curtis Mayfield on the radio. The my uncle bottom bitch Candy fired p some reefer and passed it to my uncle. Candy was my uncle top girl, she had been with him the longest, when he has all of the girls together, she is the one who gets to sit in the front seat. In the game she is a playa bottom bitch.

My uncle then passed the reefer to Honey. She was Cuban and black, Honey was from Miami, five foot two and thick. She had long jet black hair with the deep waves in it, her skin was like caramel, and it looked like honey. She was giving Candy a run for her money, my uncle pulled her about two years ago in Las Vegas at the playas ball. She left her man standing on the strip looking crazy Honey sat to the left of me, Jet was to my right, she was the thickest of them all. They called her Jet because she was a black sexy motherfucker, with short hair and eyes like a Chinese, She was from Texas, Dallas I think. I think she is new to me. Honey started to pass the reefer to Jet I grabbed it. Honey asked me what are you doing? I asked Velt could I hit it? That's what my father and I called him. He said what lil Rose? I told him that I was going through some things back here. He said something's like what? I told him that I was tripping off my mama not coming. About my father and about him coming in the middle of the night snatching me out of the city. like he did. The women looked at me like I was crazy. That was the first thing that I had said all night, Roosevelt knew that I was fast for my age. As he looked in the rear view mirror and said, go ahead lil pimping I feel you nigga. I hit it about four times and passed it to Jet and laid on back. Honey said Rose he didn't even cough or nothing. How long has this little boy been smoking?

I told her that I was a man and that I stand on my own. My father carried me as one and that I expected you to do so too., until I show you other wise. Her mouth just hung open. My uncle said, boy I hear your daddy in your voice, I miss I'm too lil Rose. I said, me too Uncle Roosevelt. We been on the road now for about four hours now, just passing the sign that said welcome to Chicago, I told Roosevelt that I wanted something to eat, we pulled in at Denny's My Uncle Tarzan I went to the restroom, and his crew was riding together, Uncle Pat and his crew were riding together. I went to the restroom, when I came back out the Ho's were just looking at me they were tripping of how my uncles were treating me. I guess thought Tarzan and Pat was going to treat me like a little boy. They didn't know that AI was the first born, I was the first grand baby to my grand mother. I was raised with them like a little brother. I was 15 years old standing at five feet already, one hundred and sixty pounds. Honey told Tarzan what I said in the car, Tarzan said Lil Rose, I said What's up playa? He said she don't know and laughed, I said now she does, I said Honey, she said what? I told her that she is still a bad Ho!!

The hold table fell out laughing. When we were sitting at the table I was sitting between Tarzan and Pat, Roosevelt was sitting at the head of the table and Candy, Honey and Jet was sitting across from us. The other cats were at another table doing their thing. I didn't know that my uncles would be the ones to mold me into the man that AI was going to become in the future. My father would not have had it any other way. For the first time I felt safe since my father had died. That was a good feeling too, when we got ready to leave Tarzan asked me if AI wanted to ride with them? I said, Shit

I'm cool on those hard leg playa. Roosevelt got the right idea, Roosevelt said to Tarzan, That's why June named him Lil Rose playa. He knows a good thing when he sees it. Tarzan told Roosevelt, man fuck you nigga and started laughing, Roosevelt told Tarzan, yo daddy nigga!

When we got in the car, ZI told Roosevelt to put in that Atlantic Starr and bump it. Honey had to say something, Boy what do you know about that? I told her I probably can show you a thing or two. She said Yeah right Nigga! I know one thing you show do talk a lot of shit. See that's the way I like it baby girl. Jet started laughing and said your daddy gave you the name didn't he, I said show you right. As we rode on down the highway I saw Honey checking me out, from the corner of her eye. I saw her because I was checking her out myself. I felt myself getting sleepy, I laid my head on Honey's chest. When I tripped off where, I was laying I set back up and looked at her, We made eye contact, she told me that I had sexy brown eyes. I told her that she was just beautiful she started to blush She asked me if I was sleepy, I said yes, she turned her body slightly toward me. She had her back up against the back seat and the door.

Then she put her hands gently around my head as she slowly pulled me over to her big breast. As we rolled listening to Atlantic Starr, she was rubbing on my back. And I was rubbing on her thigh. Roosevelt was talking to Candy about me. I heard him say, that lil Rose has been through a lot over the last few months. Candy said, Roosevelt I know can I ask you a question? Yeah baby. Can't you just see and feel his strength If I was his age I would be so scare. Roosevelt said haven't you ever heard the saying the a youngest with an old soul. They were talking about Rose, when he was little he was doing thing kids nine and ten was doing. He picked p on shit so quick until we really had to watch what we did around him. My mother use to say that Lil Rose had been here before, so that's why we treat him like we do. He's special after a while you will see. My brother started talking to him like a man to teach him understanding. When we use to lie to him June would get in our ass about that, he use to tell us that the best way to have understanding was to learn the truth. He should, I mean he will get the truth from us good or bad. It's up to lil rose to choose his path in life. Do you feel me Candy? Yes daddy I feel you, now I understand.

Everyone in the car was listening to the conversation guess Roosevelt, Candy, and Jet thought that AI was sleep. When Honey heard what my uncle was saying she looked down at me as I looked up at her. Honey knew that I was woke because I was still rubbing on her thigh and I could hear her moan as my head laid on her breast. AI know what you are thinking, how old was Honey, she was nineteen years olds Anyway stay out of my business, I'm talking to you. The owl don't hate the playa hate the game. I know you wish that you were here. I can see you. I wish you would move over some, because you are crapping my style playa. Let me get back to freaking on Honey. We had about another two and half hours before we roll into Detroit. It's about forty five in the morning, we can see the sun coming up and Detroit is in the ray of the sun. Detroit was like New York City back in the thirties through nineteen sixty eight. All that ended when Dr. King was killed, They had all the cars plants, everyone had a job, money was everywhere, When you said Detroit two things came to mind beautiful cars and Motown records, If it was number one on the charts, and the artist was black nine times out of ten it was a Detroit playa or played at. That was Detroit in it hay day, what my grand mother and uncles told me any way. I've never seen that Detroit. The Detroit that I know and learned to love was burned out, The city was like a ghost own many of the businesses was set on fire and looted in the back lash of King's Murder. A lot of the stores never came back, Then s lot of the car plants moved out of the country due to workers going on strike every year about something, Shit, I would have left too. The job situation is like to a Detroit nigga is like seeing a dog walking around china. You know it's not happening, So the men of the city took the street life to provide for their family. When that happen the game got crowded and people started killing each other over whatever. B Like clockwork the state started losing nigga fifty years at a time. When that happen a lot of playa started to move all over the bubble, they started to net work with other playas and each other. And they called this part of the game the rape, just think to understand you must look at a major city like a woman, It only take one true playa to move there mack her down, then rip her all apart. The one playa job is to learn the strong and weak points of the city. He must who the playas are Major and minor. The key is finding a playa that knows the way of the street and information on the big boys in the game. You get the pulse of the city, then come back home to regroup, Then you grab the tools of your trade and the carpenters you need to put the rape down. Don't forget that minor niggas are your ghetto pass. The money you make you bring back to Detroit to feed your people. That's the way it is in every major city there is a Detroit nigga putting the rape down and the mother fuckers are loving that cut throat nigga. I don't care where you go, Let me put it like this from Frisco to Main, all the way to Spain, From the sunshine state to the frozen state all over the bubble, a Detroit play is putting down the rape. A true Detroit playa thinks like this, from the state capital to the nation capital, from the Big Apple to the Pineapple, the earth is or turf. And we are gonna talk shit and swallow spit. Pull ho's and flash gold it's all about the paper to niggas in Detroit. This is my home, this is where AI was born, This is where my grandfather ran the streets, where David Ruffin ran the streets, Marvin Gaye, Smokey Robinson, the O'Jays, I could go on and on, You wasn't a playa in the game until you played in Detroit, Detroit made and broke great mother fuckers in the game on these streets, Now faith would have it. Now it's my time to go through a crash course in the school of hard knocks, one thing about this school you fuck up, two things are going to happen, The state will send a nigga to the moon, the other thing is these nigga don't have any problem killing you, and age is nothing. You will end up on the back of a milk carton and I Ain't laughing. We finally made it to my grandmother's house she was up early like clockwork. As soon as she saw me she said come here baby and give me a kiss. I did too and like clock work I looked in her big brown eyes and said the magic words, I Love You., She told me baby you don't know how bad I needed to hear that. Roosevelt look at Candy and said I told you that he was special. She didn't say anything she just grabbed his hand. When I stay with my Grand mother I call her mama. Mama and I walked inside to get me something to eat. She told me Boy you know where everything is, I said yes mama, My uncle Roosevelt told me that one of them would come and get me later on to take me shopping for some clothes. My Grandmother asked him where is my mother at. He told her that my mother stayed and would call her later on. My grandmother said what's going on with that girl. I went back in the house to take a bath and get some sleep. I tripped of it that AI was in my father's room, I went to sleep. When I got up later that day the phone was ringing it was Tarzan, he told me to get ready to go shopping. I flip on the TV they were talking about something big that went down in St. Louis last night. A lot of people got died and got hurt at the Adam Mark Hotel, I said to myself a lot of shit went down last night. I set back on the couch and flip through a couple more channels. Don't tell me that those nigga came down there and fucked the Adam Mark around like that, shit they never came that deep before. I have never been snatched outta bed like that before without any clothes either, shit these niggas are gangsta they fuck some nigga around. Then I heard my grand mama yell, Lil Rose bring your ass in here and clean this dame tub out! You of all people know that I don't play that shit. Then I knew that AI was home, See my Grand mama was born and raised in Detroit, she met my grand daddy in the late fifties, my grand daddy was a factory worker, in the ford plant, he was a good worker, got laid off in the early sixties, then he took all of his money he saved and open a record store, selling mo town albums, He could sell water to a whale, He had the hook up, he was getting records right from hit Ville, he knew all of the greats when they were broke and trying to make it happen. He would to tell my father and my uncles that a man should make his own money, don't work for the white man, and own your own that's the play. He was shining in the sixties; he bought a big pretty house in a nice neighborhood.

My father and uncles had what they needed and some of what they wanted. In seventy two a man came into the store to rob him, they said that he told the nigga that he wasn't giving him shit. They got into it and the man shot him three times and ran away with nothing. He fell and hit a casein lamp and the shop went p in flames. In Detroit the winters are cold and windy, the fire went through it fast, and he had no insurance. So my grand mother had to work her fingers to the bone. She said she wasn't going back to the projects and she didn't either. It took strength to hold on to what she had and raise a group of boys in the city of Detroit. When I got finished with the tub, the phone ranged I picked it p it was my mama. I asked her why she didn't come with us? She told me she had something that she had to do. She asked me if I was alright, I said, you know that I am. Then I said, how about you and Bug? She said, we are during good, I asked if I could talk to scrap, she said NO. I said why, she said that she was in Mississippi, I said, Mississippi? What are you doing down there? I'm at my mama's house I'm going to do something down here. I said, I'm cool on Mississippi, when I said that I heard a horn blowing outside. It was Tarzan, I told my mama that I had to go, I love you with all my heart, she said, the same. Then she told me to pt my grand mother on the phone. My grand mama got on the phone and I took out of the door. I was on the street with the king of the jungle, he asked me what the fuck took you so long lil Rose? I told him that I was on the phone with my mama. Then I told him that she was in Mississippi, he said, what the fuck is she doing down there in the mother fucking woods? I said, man I don't know. Then I asked him, what the fuck is this? Lil nigga, this the who's ride? Yeah because when it comes through you never know who ride it is, I started laughing and we pulled off. At the same time my mama was talking to my grand mama. My mama said Hello Big Mama, how are you doing Ann? Fine Big Mama, said, my grandmother asked why didn't you come back up here Ann? My mama said, Big Mama I wanted to go and see my mama. I can understand that, how is she doing? fine big mama. So what's up Ann? Big mama I told Rose that I wanted him to come down here and he said that he was cool. Ann you have to understand that he's a city boy. Big Mama, I know that since June passed, I have been lost he made all the moves for the family. Grand mama said, Baby, I been there when June's daddy died. Big mama, I am going to enroll in college Monday morning. Ann, what are you planning to take up? Business and marketing, that's good baby. Don't worry about Rose I got him on this end. Thanks you Big Mama that takes a lot off my mind. Baby do you need some money? No big Mama, June left me some. I am going to send Rose some money Monday, Big mama said, Baby keep that, we got him., baby get yourself together., I'll tell Rose when he gets home. Big mama, how do you think he will take it hard, but he will be alright God got us.

CHAPTER FOUR

School Days

When I got back from shopping with Tarzan, my grand mother called me to her room. She said, she had something to tell me, I said, is it s about my mama down in Mississippi? Yeah baby it is. I said is everything okay? She said, yeah baby everything is fine. She needs to do something down there to help you later in life. I said like what big mama? She said that she is going to college with the money your daddy had. I said that's cool. I asked what now I have to move down there in the woods? NO! That's what I wanted to talk to you about. You stay here with me in Detroit, I told my grand mother that was cool. She asked me if I was alright with that. I said, yes big mama. But in my heart I felt like AI had just lost my mama too, damn my daddy was already gone, now my mama is too. Then my grand mother said I didn't think you would take it so well, I smiled and walked out of the room. She called me, when I made it to her bedroom door. I turned around Monday I'm taking you to enroll you in school. I said, Alright big mama. I went to my father's room, my fault my room. My Thursday was a mother fucker well, at lease I had a three day weekend. As I looked out of the window, I tripped off going to school up here. How do these cats move?

Will I fit in? Then I started to get depressed. Then I started to trip of the school girls. Shit I started to feel better about myself. When I was shopping with Tarzan, this nigga was buying me shit I never heard off. Shit called Used jeans, I had five pair of them top and bottom in all colors. Two troop coats what the fuck was a troop coat? Some army shit, he bought me four kango bee bop hats I different color. When we I came to shoes I was lost, I got some shit called troops three pairs, Dia dora, two pairs, lattos two pairs, converse two pairs and one pair of Nike's. Man that nigga bought me a hot as triple fat goose coat. Nigga's up here was getting smoked over that mother fucker coat. That one was staying in the closet! I had some shit and all of it was high as all out doors too. Tarzan looked out for me, I needed someone at this stage in my life. I was around the house for the next two days, big mama knew I was feeling bad, one thing about her, she didn't ask come and ask me a hundred questions like most people. She did let me go through my thing my own way, I love her for that. I guess she called Roosevelt, he told me to get my ass in the shower. It was a Saturday afternoon, and sunny outside. When I made it outside Roosevelt was in money green eighty three convertible Eldora do Cadillac brougham with tan interior, A gold CC grill with the flying woman on the front and gold trimming all around the car. He had some rims on it that I never herd of, they were all gold spoke rims they were starters. Roosevelt said, that they were named Dayton's and he had them on some vogues tires. He had his name in the head rest and in big letters in the back seat. He also had green floor mats on the front and back floor. Roosevelt had niggas smiling from ear to ear when they saw that lac hit the corner in the ghetto. He had on green gators with one hundred percent cotton slacks, with a tan silk shirt short with green buttons. He also had a furry green kango hat on his head, and gold earrings gold watch, and bracelet with a do ropes with a lion head with two iced eyes on it. That nigga was clean as all out doors. When AI got in the car he asked me, What are you doing? I said nothing. He said let's go shopping. I said Tarzan took me shopping already. He said, I see that's why I'm taking you now. You were named after me lil Rose, I'm your uncle and god father right? I said alright. You got to wear what I wear. I said Nigga let's go! Man that nigga was playing freaking tales by too short. That shit was bumping too. I was rolling with neighborhood star on a sunny day in a pretty ass car. See Roosevelt was the type of nigga that always had two grand or more on him at all times. That nigga had women all over town let me tell you, he had women all over the bubble. His saying was that he was nation wide with pimping and he didn't fuck with niggas that was with that simping. Or first stop was the barber shop, when we walked in the whole shop lite up with smiles, and all you heard was What's up pimping Rose? Roosevelt said, same soup, I'm just trying to find a pretty young bitch that's down with this pimping. Niggas couldn't do nothing but smile and shake their heads. In the streets I heard from Roosevelt that a playa must always stay in character, because that is what you are judged on when the streets are watching. You will stay the same when the streets talks, the streets are always watching, and talking good are bad, so watch your moves. Roosevelt stood in the middle of the floor and said, listen up everyone AI have an announcement. Believe it or not the whole barber shop got quite; the barbers even stop cutting to hear what he had to say. This is lil Rose a pimp in process, so when you see him you see me.! So please look out for him and keep it real with him. I heard a nigga getting his hair cut say, is that your son? Roosevelt said, No pimp Sue that's June's son. Pimp Sue then told me to come here, I walked over there and Pimp Sue said, your daddy was a real nigga lil man and we go back to the beginning of time. Then he gave me a knot. I looked at Roosevelt and he shook his head yeah. Then I took it and said thanks pimp Sue. Don't worry about it I ole your old dude my life. If I can do anything for you let me know. I mean anything Rose. I didn't know what to say, but Okay and smile. Roosevelt said, pimp Sue was solid and good people. After we got our hair cut and pimp Sue got the rollers out of his head. I walked over and gave the woman who did it sixty dollars for his bill. The whole place stopped in their tracks and looked at me. The whole place was in slow motion, it seems like it took me forever to get across the floor. Even pimp Sue looked at me, She told me that Ai paid to much it was only fifty dollars. I said what baby girl you don't take tips? She said, yeah I do. She then looked at Roosevelt and once again he shook his head, Yes, Pimp Sue said Lil Playa I got that, I said that the least that Ai can do for someone that goes back with my old dude from the beginning of time playa. Pimp Sue smiled and then said, Rose I can't do nothing but tip my tip my hat to you playa. Roosevelt said, that's my boy there, this shit runs through our veins. Let's roll Lil Rose, before we left the head barber gave Roosevelt a fat ass bank roll come to find out, Roosevelt owned half of the barber shop. He then told them to put the word out about me. Now trip off this move I put down with Pimp Sue. It wasn't nothing because I used the money he gave me, well some of it. Moves, like that is what makes a playa a legend in the game. Because the barber shop was packed with playas and hustlers and they were watching. So that means that the streets were watching. And you know that they are going to talk about what they saw today in here on the streets. So the street is going to talk and every one is going to tell how they saw it go down. So that is what I mean when I say that the streets are watching and talking, you feel me on that playa? When we got to the car, Roosevelt asked me why did you do that? I said, when he said that about my old dude and gave me some money, I felt like he had love for him, so at the same time for me. That was the only way I saw that I could say Thank you. I hope that AI didn't do anything wrong Uncle Roosevelt, But it just seems right to me. Roosevelt said, Boy that move is right that is what legends are made of in the game playa. By me begin young I said, Man whatever! Turn the music up. At that time I didn't understand what AI had did. It was nothing. Then we went shopping, one thing I learned about Roosevelt he had a lot of respect all over the city. The respect that I saw was the kind that people didn't want to see nothing happen to you and would help you anyway they could. I really believed that they had love for Roosevelt and he knew it.

I asked him about it when we were getting our nails done, I asked him how did he get the respect of the people like that? He laid back in the chair with a woman doing his toes and one buffing his nails on one hand. I must say that he looked real playa in that chair. Then he answered my question, I gave them respect, It's a lot of people in the world that would like to do the things that I do, but they are afraid of the bad side of the game. I said, what about you? He said baby boy there ill be a time that you will have to make a choice in life. You must choose your path in life, I said, the good or bad path right? He said, there is no such thing as the good or bad path in life. What ever you choose to do you must stand on it good are bad. Lil Rose, you are on a path now, it up you to get what you want, and live how you want. Do you understand what I am saying? I looked at him and said, yeah I feel that there, I sat back in the chair and tripped off what the old head just laid on me. As the woman started to buff out my toe nails, I thought about my choices in life, as that reefer kicked in I just mellowed on out. He bought me some playa shit when we went shopping I had about eight fits and shoes to match. He also told me that when we roll to wear what he bought, I said okay Velt no problem. Then he told me that we had one more stop before he took me home took us about thirty minutes to get there, it was right out side the city, it was Roosevelt's house it was beautiful too. It was a two story brick home, it sat back of the street about three hundred feet behind some trees, there were no lights on the streets, if you didn't know where your were going you would have drove right passed it. We turned on to his drive way and drove through some trees, then we rolled up on his house, it was so beautiful. It was brick with white pillows in front of it, then he had row of scrubs that started from the end of the walk way and ended at the front of the house. He had big bay windows with a glass double front door. The driveway went in a circle around a big fountain, off to the side there was a three car garage. When we walked into the house there was a stair case that went to the right, I looked to my left there was the living room, When you walked into it you had to walk down three steps to go enter it, it was all white, the couch was a wrap around leather, it was backed up against a wall that was the front of the house, So the couch was facing the back of the house, where the glass windows which were the length of the living room. I could just imagine how beautiful it would be when it showed. He had white carpet and a big glass coffee table that sit on a gold panther, under the table he had a tan bear rug, so when you sit on the couch you could see through the coffee table and see the tan bear rug, the tan on the bear matched the panther, that was holding up the glass table. That was some fly shit! He also had a fire place with panthers sitting on each side they were gold too, Then he had an oak cased book case that wrapped around the wall, it started at the glass and ended at the glass. I shouldn't have to explain the rest of the house, do I? If you said yes look at Miami vice it comes at eight o'clock on Friday nights on NCB that should do it for you there. I went to the kitchen and open the box to see what this balling ass nigga had to eat. Then I heard a sweet voice say Hello Rose, I closed the door and standing behind it was honey's fine ass. She had a red teddy on with her butt hanging out without a bump on it. She had her hair down it hung pass her shoulders, as I looked down she also had on a pair of red high heels shoes with red lip stick on, I said, what's up then open the door back up in her face. She asked me how did she looked, I said, baby girl you cool, she said what you mean I'm cool nigga, I told her honey pass me with that bull shit if you ain't talking about cooking something get the fuck on. She said, fuck you nigga and turned around and walked away. I looked around the door that ass was shaking, then Jet's black ass walked in and said, what's up! I said what's up blacker than me, she had on a white teddy with white pumps, She was a black thick sexy mother fucker, she put on an apron and asked me what did I want to eat. Then Honey walked back into the kitchen and told Jet not to fit me shit. I told Honey that she was mad because all she knew how to fit was toast. I really see that Cuban in her, Jet didn't make it any better by saying, Rose I see you know her. Man, Honey hit the roof, I had her number now. I was glad that I was high. Because I would have really been caught up on what she had on, and she would had got. I heard someone call my name, I said, Yeah! Lil Rose, Lil Rose, it was Candy. there was a set of stairs in the kitchen. They came right down out of the ceiling like a circle from up stairs to down stairs. When Candy came all you could see first was her pretty feet. She was wearing some pink heels with fur on the front of them, she took a few more steps then you cold see her long coco butter brown legs, it seems like they ran for days. She took a few more steps down the stairs, I cold see then that she had teddy on also. Hers was pink with white lace, she also had long hair was sandy brown. She stood at five feet ten inches, she was tall and thick, she was a little darker right under her butt. She was bow legged just enough and could stand back in her legs. She had tight Chinese eyes and a small cute nose. She didn't have no problems showing off her body, she did most of the recruiting for Roosevelt, nigga don't look for that in the game. When ho's are on the track and Roosevelt pulls up they turn their heads and walk away. Because if you make eye contact and she holds it, two things are going to happen. One she is digging you, and she is trying to choose up on your pimping. Two is if she holds eye contact, she could be put under pimp arrest and the pimp she is eye balling, he can take her money or any other thing of wealth. When her man comes to get his paper, and she has been under pimp arrest, he is gonna beat her ass. And bust her feet to get the money right. It's a cold game but it's fair. Candy told me that Roosevelt wanted me to come up stairs. I told her I was waiting on my cheese burger and French fries. She said that someone would bring it up to you I. I told her to come closer to me I wanted her to do something for me. She said, like what Lil Rose? I told her to make Honey to bring it to me. She said why Honey.? I said that she is mad at me right now. Candy please, she said Ok boy. Before she stood all the way up I kissed her on the check. She smiled and hit me on my butt and told me to go on up, your uncle is waiting on you.

I walked by Jet I smacked her on her butt and said thanks for cooking me something to eat. I went on up to Roosevelt's room, when I walked in I called Velt, he said I'm in the tub. I told him that I am not coming in there. He said, Nigga bring your big head ass in here boy. I said yo daddy had a big head nigga. He laughed and said you look just like him Lil nigga. I said Fuck you Velt and we both laugh at each other. As I looked around the room, I saw a painting of Velt and Candy it was tight too. The room was gold and green all the way through it. They had a king size bed with big pillows, the covers was dark green with gold leafs in it. They had the pillow cases to match the wallpaper, was dark green with gold leafs in it. The boarder were gold green leafs the windows were the length of the room. I walked through there to the bath room. Let me say that the bathroom was a big room. I had to open a double glass door with gold handles. What I saw fucked me up, the Nigga was sitting down in a tub that could seat four with no problem. Bubbles and looking at a flat screen television that was in the wall. Telling me to pass him a light to fire up a fat ass Jay, Then he said, nigga you don't know nothing about this. I said about what? He said Scare Face then he turn it on the TV. It was at the part when Scar Face told Chico to get the Ya Yo, I told him that was me and my old dude shit. He said, I know it was Rose

Then Honey walked in with my food on a platter. Then she sat it down in front of me, AI told her thank you, and she smiled. When she started to walk away, I grabbed her hand and pulled her close to me and whispered in her ear. I told her that she didn't have to ask me how she looked, because she already knows that she is beautiful. She was smiling from ear to ear. Then I smacked her on her ass and told her to get me some salt and pepper. She gave me one of those looks her eyes got tight and her jaws got tight I learned that from my old dude, he did my mama like that for years, and she loved it. It took her about ten minutes to come back, all of my fries were gone, and she looked at me and asked Rose do you want some more? I said, No I'm okay thanks for asking, Roosevelt asked her to show me the guess room. She grabbed my hand and pulled me to the room, it was right beside hers. As we were walking all I could do was look at that tale, Honey was bad. Then Candy came in and said this is your room now when I was out there. I could see Honey's eyes light up, then she said, Nigga now I have got to deal with you. I said that you know that you like me. She said that you are a little boy. I said, I'm bigger than you all over, She looked around and said, boy you couldn't handle this, I would have your nose open, you would be on my heels around here. I said, like you are on mine right now. She snatched her hand away from me and walked away then candy came and told me that I will be staying here to night. I said, I'm keeping it real I damn near killed myself that night thinking about Honey, Jet, and Candy in their titties. I damn near ran out of lotion. Honey was only nineteen in age, she was about fifteen in the mind. When it comes to thinking, I believe I'm faster than her, I can out think her, shit we will see. It's Monday morning I'm in the office of the school., they told my grand mother that I had missed to many days of school in St. Louis and would have to do the seventh grade over the summer school with help. But that I could still get to know the teachers for next year. It wasn't long before the summer break started, this means may. In the next three weeks I got cool with a dude named Sunny Boy, He had to do the seventh grade over too, that skipping caught up with us. It was about three months, I asked big mama where was Pat, she said that he was in Seattle working, I said working! She said yeah baby that's what they say, they think that I this morning baby. I said, I know that's not true.

Chapter Five

The Birth Of Rosewood

(Three years later)

The year is 1989. I'm seventeen years old now. I'm six feet one inch, two hundred and ten pounds. I still live with big momma and only talk to momma on the phone and see her on thanksgiving and Christmas. She is doing good. I'm proud of her. She only needs one more year then she will be finished with a B.A in business. You could say there were two people on that education. She made copies of her books for me and when she took a test I took one too. I did better than she did on a couple of test. I have been in college for three years now, I only need one more year and I will have a B.A in business too. But school just let out for the summer and I will have the whole summer to myself. My momma asked me to come home for the summer again. I had to tell her I love you but I couldn't do it again. I told her to do her thing I'll get at her later. Do you remember Sunny boy? Come to find out when Pat came back, his mean boy was Sonny's old dude. Sunny and I became tight like me and my cuzzin Scrap. I haven't seen Scrap in the last three years. I use to call but Kim and my momma fell out, and when I would call she would rush him off the phone. But that's still my dog. Let me give you the low down of my uncles over the last three years. You better listen up cause I'm going to say this fast, ok. They acted a damned fool, not damn but DAMNED fool. Let me start off with Tarzan, that nigga went to Kansas city and robbed about thirty dope houses. Then he gave the dope to Pat for a little bit of nothing. Then Pat would pick the work up in Kansas city and go sell it in Iowa, Nebraska, North and South Dakota. Man them niggas was putting the rape down. Their money was right too. Roosevelt damn near got locked the fuck down in Vegas about eight months ago. They had a ring of pimps that got busted selling that work. They were making deals with the F.B.I for lesser time. Someone told on Roosevelt. Roosevelt never sold work, but niggas in the street didn't know that, so they put them boys on Velt. See Velt use to pimp hard back in the day, his goal was to stack his paper and go into business with people he knew. So he was a co-owner of five barber shops in three different states. He also had money tide up in two clubs and four detail shops. When he was nineteen he went to barber college. The reason was to meet women, but he saw a hustle there and jumped on it and got his license. See the barbers only get cash, that's one of the only trades like that in the country. See when you get that license it comes with a F.I.N number. That lets u spend cash on anything and I mean anything playa. Let me give you some game, a F.I.N number is a federal identification number it's like a social security card. When u spend over ten thousand dollars on something you give them the F.I.N number they type it in and that goes to the F.B.I office, that shows that you have the right to spend cash like that. By me sharing information like that with you. That should show you the level of thinking Roosevelt is on, that's the shit we call the game. So he had a few high priced tricks all over the bubble. So when he came to town he would have Candy drop them a line and they would drop that paper, he's in Vegas doing his thing, he was in pimp mode at this time. Now he only goes in pimp mode in the city where there are hair shows going down. That was of thinking saved his ass, cause when Candy, Honey, and Jet dropped off the cash they would jump down on him. He had a little bit under thirty thousand dollars on him when they got him. But Roosevelt never came out of character he stayed clam, cool, and collected. The police and the F.B.I thought that they had did something, they didn't know that they were fucking with one of Detroit's finest true playa of the game. They took pictures of the money all over the table, slapping each other on the back, and saying good job. They locked Candy, Honey< and jet up. They split them up into different rooms but they all told the same story, then they tried to get Roosevelt to roll over on some playas in the game. Roosevelt told them that he is a business man he also told them how many barber and beauty shops he owned. The F.B.I agent said that they knew all that and asked why did you have all that money on you? I know why cause you're a mother fucking pimp and we have your ass red handed he said. So what do you want to do Velt asked. Listen, Roosevelt I know you are a pimp, we busted you selling drugs and they told on you. Roosevelt said, Damn man I can answer the second question first. The agent said sure. Am I a pimp? Yes I am a pimp but my barber and beauty shops are my hoes. My answer to the first question is, I had that money on me to buy some products for my business. "From where?" the F.B.I man asked? From the hair show Velt told him. Then he told the man to go and get something to write with. When the man came back he gave him the information for the hair show, then he gave him his F.I.N number. Then he told him that he wasn't saying anything else. An hour later Candy, Honey, Jet, and Roosevelt was out, with the thirty thousand on him. They were on the first thing smoking back to Detroit. After that he gave up on pimping, niggas in the street couldn't believe what was going on. They made a bet on how long he could stop pimping. Pimp Sue said that the game was going to be calling him. That was eight months ago. Candy, Honey, and Jet still live with him and still do business for him. But its all good now, he really making paper now. Well that sums up the last three years. One day it was raining outside Velt wanted me to spend the night but I wanted to get some rest because Honey been on my heels to last year, so I told him I was cool. Honey looked at me like I was crazy, then said Lil rose you're a little boy. I know you are afraid of me, but that's cool. I told her "yeah right baby girl. I'll see you later hooker." She smiled then kissed my hand, then said "I'll be thinking about you and I know you'll be thinking about me. I told her "Hell no take your ass home." and walked out the house. I went on in and lay in the bed. After a while I found myself looking at the ceiling, bored out of my mind. I started looking through my old dudes books for something to read I ran across some books that would change my life for the better. There were two books, one was named The Art of War, the other was named The Black Prince. They were both by the same guy named Micaville. I ended up staying in my room two days reading the gangster bible. Part one and two. When I was reading I saw parts of it in high light. I guess this was the moves that he mastered for the game. There was a lot of useful information in these books. When I was young my old dude would always say that, information was the power of the world. He would ask me "what was power?" I would say "money". He would say "no its information because without it you couldn't have all the money in the world but without information you can't invest in business or stocks and bonds. Getting paper is the easy part, growing it to work for you is the hard part." Then he asked the question again and I couldn't say anything but information. My old dude use to drop seeds on me like all the time. He always said that he was raising a thinking man, now I see where he was coming from. I have seen a lot of people that had other people thinking for them. Don't get me wrong to each its own I never understood it. I was raised to think for myself. A man must think for his family and self. Then the phone rang, I picked it up "hello", "what's up man? This is Velt. What are u doing nigga? I haven't heard from you I called Pat and Tarzan, they both said that they haven't heard or talked to you in two days." Velt calm down play boy. I have been in my room reading for the past two days. Velt said "boy that must be some good shit to keep you in the house for two days. What are you reading?" I told him "you not ready for this shit here play boy." He laughed and asked again, I told him "the art of war and the black prince." Velt said that I had the right shit in my hand." It's powerful information to a thinking man and a death ticket to a fool that can't think for himself. Do you feel what I'm saying?" I said "yes, you know I do because if I didn't you know that I was cool on it." Velt said yeah I know. I said "Velt man you don't have to worry about me man." He said "lil rose I love you lil nigga, Im always thinking about you. I see you as my son." I said thank you I don't hear that much. That's why you called me? Fuck no I called to ask you if you wanted to go to the playas ball? I said damn right! Where is it going to be at? He said Hollywood CA. so get ready. I'll pick you up in the morning. I asked who all is going? Velt said, Candy Honey, and Jet. I asked him are we driving? He said no we are flying out there. You don't have a problem with that. I said I never rode a plane before. That is going to be cool, make sure you get my seat next to Honey, ok? He looked at me and said, I got u lil player. Then he asked me what color was I planning to wear to the ball? I told him black, yellow, and gold. He said isn't that what you bought last week in chi town with Pat? I said, you know it play boy. I'm going to be so clean they might close the club down for a clean violation. He laughed and said, I got to see what you put together boy. I asked him to make share he bring me some ear rings and a chain. He said, that he had something els to do today. Then I asked him to put Honey on the phone. He said that she was sleep. I said so! He laughed then I could hear him calling her in the back ground. She yelled, tell who ever the fuck is on the phone, that I'm sleep! He told her that it was Rose on the phone. Then I heard her say, tell him to hold on. When she finely put up the phone, I could hear that she just woke up. I said, hello baby did I wake you? She said yeah you did. Then I asked her if she wanted me to call her back later on? She said, hold on Nigga, where the fuck have you been the last couple of days? I asked her, was I with you. She said no. then I told her, so don't worry about where the fuck I was! Just worry about playing your spot. You acting like I'm your man are something. It don't cost a dime to stay out of mine playa. I could hear her getting mad. Then she said, nigga what the fuck do you want? Then I asked her, honey were you worried about me? You already know what I want. She said, what's that? Then I told her, I want you! I have been thinking about you for the last few days. She didn't say anything for a minute. Then she asked me, is that why you called me this morning? I said, yeah that's one of them. I had to get that off my chest. The other thing was that I need you to take me to a couple of places, if you don't mind. I could hear her smile through the phone. Then she said, Rose I will do anything for you. I said, you would. Then I heard her say, that's what I said. I got quite then told her, baby I didn't know that you felt that way about a playa. Her tone got soft then she said, baby you had me a long time ago. Then I told her to bring her mother fucking ass on then! She got hot and told me fuck you, then she hung up the phone. I thought about calling back then I said fuck it. Then I started back reading that gangsta shit. About twenty minutes later the phone rang. I didn't pick it up because ever time I lose myself off in to this book someone calls. A couple of minutes later the phone rang again. Big momma picked it up and said that the phone was for me. When I picked it up it was Honey. She told me that she was on her way. I told her to bring me some money and not to ask velt for any either. Then I asked her to put Velt on the phone. When he picked up I told him not to give Honey any money for me. He told me okay my nigga, then we hung up the phone. Then again I tried to get back off into my book. Then the phone rang again, I picked it up this time and it was Honey. I said Bitch what? She said nigga that was some cold shit there. I told her that the game was cold but it was fair. Then I asked her if she was coming or what? Because I can call Pat, or Velt to come get me. She said, nigga I'm coming but I don't have any money. I said, baby don't worry I can call Pat, or Tarzan. Then she told me that she was on her way. Then she asked me why did I need some money? I told her that I needed to go shopping for the playa ball. She told me that she asked Velt to bring me to the ball. I told her that was cool, but right now you need to bring your ass on. An hour later Honey showed up at the door. When big mama opened the door Honey asked her where I was? Big mama told her that I was in my room reading a book. Honey knocked on my door. I asked who is it? She said, Honey. I told her to come on in. when she opened the door I was setting at my desk with my back to her. When she walked in I said, what's up, baby thanks for coming to get me. At this time my back was still to her and my nose was in my book. She said, Rose I told you that I would do anything for you. I was still reading my book. I was listing to every word she was saying. I said yeah, just to be saying something. She walked up behind me and kissed me on my neck. Then she ran her hands down my shoulders onto my chest. She had something in her right hand. I had my eyes closed. I felt it up against my skin on my chest. She was still kissing my neck. Then she whispered into my ear. She said, Rose will you please be my man. I did everything in my power to trap you. But instead you have trapped me off into your web. I give up will you please have me as your woman. Then I asked her you chose me? Then she told me, Rose I love you. Then I told her to get right then and drop it likes its hot. Do you remember when I said that I felt something on my skins? She dropped it in my lap, it was a knot. Better know as a fat bank roll. All together it was thirty five hundred dollars. When I spent around in my chair from my desk. Honey was standing there in some daisy duke shorts on that was so tight hugging her hips, and you could see her ass cheeks hanging out of the bottom of her shots. She also had on a yellow follower low cut top on, that was tied into a knot. So you can see her belly bottom. She had her hair pulled back into a pony tail. The only make up she wore was lip stick. She was so beautiful to me and she wanted to be in my life. The way I saw it was. I was the youngsta and it was suppose to be the other way around. When I tripped off of it she was crying. I had never seen that side of her before. I always saw the street side of her. The hip, slick, strong side of her. I told her to come here. She walked up sit on my lap and put her head on to my chest. As I rubbed her back she rubbed my leg. Then I said, this is how I we met. She looked up and said, that this feels so right to me. Then I kissed her on her forehead and said, I would love to be your man. I see it as a blessing on my behalf. She pulled herself together and told me lets go. I put on my shoes and we went outside. She gave me the keys and said it's yours. She was rolling an eighty six B.M.W, blue with tan interior. I just looked at her and said to myself, damn we haven't even had sex. We jumped in and rolled out to handle my business. When we got out to the car she opened the door, and when I got in she closed the door. To the streets I was pimping, and Honey was my bottom hoe. When we got on the highway I asked her about uncle Roosevelt, so what are we going to tell him. She said "baby he already know." I said "how is that?" Last year he picked up on how I felt about you, he asked me how I felt and I told him I was in love with you. "What did he say?" I asked. He just looked at me and said "I must give you another spot in the family." "What spot is that?" I asked. She said that she had become the runner of the family. I pick up and drop off coast to coast. I said "What did you move?" she said money baby only money. I asked "So how did Candy take it, you taking her spot?" "It fucked me up, she said that I had her blessing." Honey said. She also told me that Candy and Velt see me as the son, and that Candy told Velt about the way I feel about you. At first Vet said that I wasn't the one for you, that he wanted you to choose your own woman. Candy told him "Honey is the baby of the family and her being a hooker was going to stop if he chose her." After Honey told Velt how she felt about me that changed her whole roll in the game. She started seeing parts of the game she has never seen before. Candy pulled up on her and told her that Velt is training her to move for me as my bottom bitch in the game. Candy took Honey under her wing and became her teacher on the ways to please me. She also showed her how to be my extra set of eyes in the streets. She taught Honey how to look for snakes in my presence. I asked her how she could see that? Honey said "when you are handling your business and a nigga is trying to pick me up or look at me on the side he's a snake." I must let you know to watch him at all times, cause a nigga will kill you to get you out the way. They'll tell the police on you it's a lot of shit in the game that I didn't know. But rose I'm ready now, they have been molding me for the last year. I said "That's why you stop tripping with me on every little thing." She said "yes, and the only reason I use to trip was because I liked you and that was the only way I could get you to see me." I told her "I use to watch you all the time." She said "I couldn't tell." I laughed and said "you weren't going to know either that was the plan." She said "it worked too." "When was the last time you had sex?" I asked. She said "with someone." I said yeah. She said a year ago. I told her to get the fuck outta here. She said for real boy. The deal was that I had to wait for you. I said for me? She said yeah for you. I asked her "who came up with that?" She said it was Candy who said that. She took me to the doctor to get checked out. I passed with flying colors. Then she took me to the sex store and bought me some things to handle my business. I said handle your business, right. She said when you use to spend the night I use to do my thing. I told her me too. She said I know I use to watch you then go do my thing. When we got to Velt's house I went right to the living room where he was. He asked me what was up. I said you tell me pimping. He asked was your choice yea or na. I said yeah. He looked at me and said that I made a good choice, then shook my hand. Then he said that it was up to me how I move with that, and that he also had my back. He said "Rose you should know by now that I see you as my son." I said "Roosevelt we have always been tight, you was my guy when I was little." He said "I know lil rose, boy you need to think of a new name cause you've out grown that one." You know I'm pimping Rose. When you do so make sure it fits you playa. I said I will. He said you will be sixteen in September, I n my book your grown, you are old enough to drive legally and go to the pen for the rest of your life. So please watch what you do and say now, cause it's on you out there in the streets. You know that she watches and talks, she can make and break you. At this time I could hear the girls in the kitchen laughing and jumping up and down. I looked around the corner and Candy was hugging Honey and Honey was crying again. I pulled up on Velt and asked him what was going on in the kitchen. He looked at me and said lets go outside and take a walk. He slide the glass door back and we stepped off to the deck by the pool. Then he said "Honey is a part of you." I said me. He said "yes, when they see her they see you, she has been around in the game for a minute. Even though she is twenty two she knows a lot and when she met you she saw that you had the game in you. Every ten to fifteen years a great one is born. Rose I think you might be the one, she sees it in you and she went through allot before you. Then it was still your choice, you could have said no. But every great man needs a good woman behind him. I said that I know that you got her together. He said you need to thank Candy, she put that work in. I said okay and I went back into the house and headed towards the kitchen. I saw Candy and I said thank you for giving me a gift so beautiful and true. She said Rose you made it happen, it was all on you and about you. She will only go as far as you go as long as she's with you. I told Candy that I felt that in my heart. I also said that I was going all the way to the top. Two days past, the playas ball is tonight, this is my first playas ball. Honey had on a black see through dress, with a black flower prints all over it. It was low cut at the top and had splits on both sides. Honey had her hair down passed her shoulders, she had it deep conditioner. When she do that her hair holds deep waves in it till she washes it out. I had on a black summer blazer with a pair of percent cotton black slacks, with a yellow vest on with black diamond's on it and a long sleeve shirt. Slick yellow tie with a slick blazer hanky. I also had some yellow gaiters on with a black dobe that also had a black and yellow feather in it. I must say we were clean. Roosevelt, Candy, and Jet was wearing red and gold. They were clean as all out doors. Velt order us a limo to go to the ball in. It was also black. Honey was all over me sense I told her that I was going to be her man. She has eying mind at me sense we got here, because Velt has been taking me around to meet other mad playa's in the game from all over the bubble. I met playa's that were living legends in the game, even some of them knew my name. They heard about what happen to pimp sue and I in the barber shop. A lot of them know my old dude. I did really see my old dude deep in the game like this. I always saw him as d boy for the ones that don't know a D boy is a dope dealer. I'm finding more out about my old dude, the deeper I get in this shit we all call the game. When we made it back to the hotel honey had my weed rolled for me and something to drink. Velt and I was gone about a day and half. We were up net working the hold time. I was so sleepy. I went straight to the shower and then to bed. Honey came in fucking with me. I told her that I needed to get some rest and to please stop talking to me. Then I heard Candy tell Honey to get her ass out of there fucking with me. See Honey never seen this part of the game before. It was new to her to at the other playa's balls she ever been too she was a ho. She only knew what she needed to know. But now Candy has put her under her wing. She has been telling her what I have been doing since we have been here. Then she told her that I have been up meeting with people for the last couple of days. He really needs to get his rest.

As we walked in the ball there were so many beautiful women there of all colors. I must say myself there were also a lot of niggas that were clean as a motherfucker. They had the tables set up by city, so you were surrounded by the playas, pimp's and hustlers from your city. I asked Velt about that, he said "he said they did it like that so you could enjoy yourself with your own people. The other reason is if you win an award they call you and your city. Cause it's a lot of playas with the same name." Then if a playa from another city has heard about you and he only knows your name or the name of your city, this helps us hook up in the game. In so many words its putting a face with the name. At the playas ball they give out awards for best dressed, best dance, best mouth piece, and the most important pimp of the year. They had a mc to host the ball, theirs was Pimp Sue he's a Detroit playa. The first one I ever met, now he's at my first playas ball. Something special might happen tonight. As the night went on the playas from Las Vegas was shinning like stars tonight. Roosevelt won best dressed, now there are two awards left. Best dance and Pimp of the year. The contest I got in was the two step, the only reason that happened is because Honey wanted to dance. When we entered it I had to give them a name I said "Rosewood". I was talking to the lady that was taking the names down when I said "Rose" Honey was talking to me at the same time I told her would you please be quit. Then the lady asked me what city was

I from I said "Detroit". At the time I didn't trip off that my name tag said Rosewood. When we were dancing Honey told me what it said. She also told me that the name fit me too. I must say I can two step my ass off, I learned how in St. Louis. Every city has their own two step and the way they do it. I mix mine with Detroit and St. Louis. The rest of the cats on the floor was looking at me and Honey. Since she was smaller than me I could do anything that came to mind. When we made it back to the tables, I had playas raising their glasses to me and tipping their hats. My uncle said boy that was a move of a legend, you the one. Honey was smiling from ear to ear, she likes every ones eyes are on her. Velt looked at my name tag and said "Rosewood it fits you and I never heard a playa with that one there. Before I could tell him what happened on the name deal, Pimp Sue called the winner of the best dance contest "ROSEWOOD from Detroit city" the ball stood up like I was the pimp of the year or something. I made my way to the stage, Pimp Sue said "Lil Rose you are your own man now your name will pop all over the bubble now." then he turned the mic on and said that we went way back and talked about the way we meet in the barber shop. Then he said "playas I would like to introduce Mr. Rosewood from Detroit Mi. The whole place stood up and took their hats off to me. Pimp Sue then asked me why they call me Rosewood. I took the mic and said "because my thoughts and conversation are delicate like a rose, but at the same time my character and my stashers is solid like mahogany wood with two d's for a double dose of this pimping. Pimp Sue said I should have gotten in the mouth piece contest too, we all laughed. I got the award and went back to the table. Detroit had two awards to take back home. I saw that Roosevelt was proud of me, Candy and Jet were too, but Honey had her chest stuck up more than mine. The playas from Vegas called me over there and gave me their number, and told me they would like for me to come visit any time to talk about business. They bought me a bottle and sent it to my table. By the time I made it back to my table there were a lot of bottles and cards on it. On my way back hoes was coming from everywhere, Honey step right in front of me and said she was the bottom ho. I grabbed her hand and went to the table. They called Playa of the year it was a playa by the name of Moon from Miami. When he was on the mic he said that he would like to welcome me to the game, and that he would like to welcome me to Miami so we could talk about things. I took my hat off and raised my glass to him. At that time Velt found his card on one of the bottles and handed to me. I raised that up twas on the way back to the hotel Velt said the award couldn't have fell no better than that. You won right before the Pimp of the year and they made you a star, you cool Rosewood.

CHAPTER SIX

Now Comes The Rain

We have been back from los angles about a week now. The word about the playa ball passed through the street like wild fire. My name was popping in every major city in the United State. I know because playa were getting at Roosevelt all week long. When we were at the ball people kept asking for my card, but I didn't have one at the time. So I used Velt card and put my name on it. One thing I must say is that I must have pulled a playa move. Better yet, like Velt always say, that was a move there that makes legends in the game. Every nigga that call was asking for Rosewood to come to town so we could talk about some business. Velt pulled me to the side and set me down. He wanted to talk to me about my choices in the game. He told me that the next three months were going to be the most important time for me in the game. People will come to you with a lot of sweet ass deals. Everything that shines isn't gold. When I looked at him I smiled and shook my head to let him know that I understood everything he was telling me. These are the ties that will be with you all through the game he said. For good or bad, like I said, good or bad play. He moved closer towards me and said, look these will be your contacts, I like to call them life lines in the game. First of all what kind of a hustler do you plan on being? I said I wanted to be a playa that's three hundred and sixty-five degrees in the game. I want to be well connected in the game. I would love to do business all over the bubble if possible. Something like you Uncle Roosevelt. The plan is to stand on my own two feet in the white man's business world, as a black business owner like my old dude and his and your old dude. He said poppa Rose still lives in all of us. I hear him coming out of you now, that's a beautiful thing we are still living his dreams. I said it's all about the paper. That's the bottom line nephew. He said, Now, the bad thing in your life line in the game is this, you have to keep your ear to the ground. Because if it's one of your life lines is going to war your need to know about it before it goes down. If you don't you could be dealing with the one he is at war with. These niggas be so gun happy, they could smoke you and then put the word out that you were working for the other cat. Another bad thing about your life lines is that if the police is on them niggas and you don't know about it. Shit you might as well go down to the police station pull your dick out and pee in the sergeant's cup while it's still in his hands. I said nigga are you crazy. He moved to the edge of his chair and leaned forward towards me, now we were nose to nose. Velt says to me baby boy this is the most important information I have learned in the game. You must know the moves of the niggas you fuck with before they do it. Then he asked what do you know about the game of chess? I said nothing. Rose I thought you were reading The Art of War? I am reading it I said, well did you get to the part where he's talking about war and chess? I said yes, he told me give me your word about something. I said about what? He said that you will not step your foot in the game till you beat him five times in a row at the game of chess. If I won four then lost the fifth I would have to start all over. The way I saw it, I would be playing for my independence in the game and as a man. My old dude was a Scarface fan, he said that the best line in the movie was when Scarface said the only thing I have in this world is my balls and my word. That was the real shit in the movie. I gave Velt my word and put it to my old dude soul to stay true to it. He pulled out a board and the pieces, and I read the rules while he was rolling up the weed. He told me to put down the paper, I'm going to show you like your father showed me. He called Candy, and told her to fix him something to drink. I said me too. He said hold the fuck up playa. Candy started to walk off, he asked her what the fuck was she going to do. She said I'm going to fix you and Rose a drink. Bitch I didn't tell you to fix him a drink did I? She said no you didn't daddy. He said then go do what I said do, then she moved on. He looked at me and said, Rosewood I found that to be real disrespectful playa. In the future if a playa don't ask don't speak on. I said, pimping please forgive me for stepping out of character. In the future I would hope that you wouldn't find my movements in a disrespectful manner. He said I feel you Rosewood we good pimping. When I asked Candy to fix me a drink the game of chess had started before I even knew how to move the knight. He knew I would ask, he could have check mated me on the board and in the streets. Because I was in the wrong and it's that simple to get dead on the board and in the game. Velt laid on back in the chair and lit up the weed. He tried to pass it to me and I looked at his ass crazy as a motherfucker. Then I laid back in my chair, I wanted some bad as a motherfucker too. Then I remembered Honey had some so I called her to the living room. When she came in I asked her to make me drink and roll up a couple of jays. She asked what kind of drink I told her some hen dog then smacked her on the ass. Velt told me to hit the weed he had, I told him I will never go down again like that playboy.

I'm going to keep it real between you and I Velt hurt my feelings when he came to me like that, that day. I know he was right by doing so he was getting me ready for the game, but I never got over that. I backed up off my uncle, it never was the same. When Honey came back with my drink I asked her to go get my coat and keys, I was going to handle some business. Then I told her to grab some clothes she was coming with me. Shit you know Roosevelt is my cat, I just need some time to think about my choices in life. He put a lot on my mind today, then that move there about the drink that was some smooth shit there. Can you feel me now, Honey and I got in the car and went downtown to a nice hotel. She got us a room for a couple of days, when we got to the room I had Honey run me a bubble bath. I went to the window and looked out, the view was beautiful cause we were on the twenty-second floor I could see the whole city. It was dark and the whole city was lit up. I stood there and tripped off Honey this was our first time alone since we hooked up. I know she tripped off of it, I wonder why she didn't say anything about it. I told her to come here, when she came over I told her to look out the window. She turned toward the window, as she was talking about how beautiful the view was I put my arms around her waist as I stood behind her. I softly whispered in her ear and told her I know a view that looks way better than this one. She bit her lip and said what, I turned her toward me I looked down in her pretty brown eyes and said "you're the most beautiful thing I ever seen in my life." I could see tears coming to her eyes as she looked up at me. Her skin was so soft and smooth, as I slowly slide my hand down the back of her arm. She said "Damn boy the tub is still on." And she ran to the bathroom. I asked her was everything alright in there, and she said yeah baby. Baby sounded so sweet coming out of her mouth, then she said that it was ready for me. I took off my clothes and jumped in the tub, the water was hot but it felt so good. Honey just stood there looking at me, I wish I could read her mind right now. I asked her that if she didn't mind would she wash my back? She said baby I don't mind. She said I would do anything for you and I mean anything too. I asked her what made you feel like this towards me? She said baby every man I've ever known only wanted one thing from me. I said what, like I didn't already know the answer. Then she said it Pussy that's what it's all about. You made me laugh and then turn right around and make me mad. If you saw me going through a thing, you seemed to find the right thing to do or say. Then when you knew I was alright later on you acted like nothing happened. You took the time to get to know my dreams in life, I could see in your eyes that you really cared about how I felt. I sat back and just watched how you moved around playas in the house and in the streets. They see it in you. I said they see what, she said baby there is something special about you. You do and say things that will make people attracted to you, like a super star. Roosevelt always use to tell us to watch you, I said why. He always said that you were a legend at work she said. He says that at your age you could be at the top of your game at the age of twenty-five. I said twenty-five, yeah that's what he said baby.

When Candy told him how I felt about you, he said that I wasn't fast enough to keep up with you in the game. He also said that that I would be on so much bullshit that I would fuck around and get you killed in the streets. Velt loves you Rosewood, after all that shit I went through it was still up to you to choose me. In this game women choose the men. Baby just trip off what happened at the playas ball, I have been to a lot of them and that Ain't never happened. The only person that gets love like that is playa of the year. You moved the crowd more than the nigga who won the big one. He couldn't do nothing but respect you, he was playa of the stage but you were playa of the year on the floor where it counts. What went down there made you a legend in the game already.

When they hear the name Rosewood just watch how their face lights up and they jump on your nuts. Just watch. Then out the blue she said that she would see me when I get done. I said okay, then I heard Luther Van dross playing in the bed room. I got out of the tub and walked in the room, there she was standing there looking out the window with her back towards me. She had a glow to her skin tonight, she had let her hair down wearing a red summer dress it was short and stopped about three inches above the knee. Then she had some red open toe heels on that had a strapped around her calf and up to her knee, and her nails were painted red too. Honey is short, but right now she looks like she has long legs. As I walked up behind her I could smell her perfume it was something sweet. Whatever it was it made the top of my head start to burn. I put my right hand on her left shoulder and moved it slowly back to the right. Her skin was so warm and smooth, I moved her hair from her neck and left shoulder and put it on the right. Then I slowly put my dark arms around her waist and pulled her body to mine nice and slow. She tried to fight a little bit, then she stepped back towards me. I could feel her butt against my body, it was so soft I could feel myself getting hard. She could too I could hear her moan real soft under her breath. I moved my hands from her waist and slide them down her soft beautiful body. I started kissing her neck she said Rose your lips are so soft, I whispered in her ear that she was beautiful, smart, and soft.

I started to move my hands back up her body and raised her dress, she took it on herself to open her stands a little wider and leant her chest against the glass. She put her right hand on the glass and turned her head to the left to look at me. I rested her dress on her back and she had on a red lace g-string. Honeys butt was perfect, she had hips and her legs were strong. She didn't have any stretch marks on her butt and she was shaved nice and clean. I put my hand between her legs, she was so hot and wet. I looked at Honey and her eyes were closed I felt her body shaking. I started to move my hand back and forth between her legs, I could see Honey starting to bite her bottom lip. I leaned forward and put my free arm around her waist. She took my hand with her left hand and had me rub under her left breast. She told me to move the hand that was in between her legs faster and I did. She started breathing really hard. She threw her other hand against the glass, now there both on the glass. Honey started to call my name, my hand was so hot and wet. Then I saw Honeys legs get weak she all most fell but she caught herself. Her body started shaking real bad then she lost her motherfucking mind!

She started screaming, shit it felt like she was pissing in my hand, she wanted me to stop but I kept on going. I held her little ass up for about ten minutes, she lost her legs. Honey started to cum back to back she was crying telling me that she loved me and not to stop. She had cum running down both of the insides of her legs. My hand was so sticky and my shit was rock hard. I laid her on the bed her eyes were still closed, and she was on her back with a crazy ass smile on her face. I took off her wet g-string and put her legs on my shoulders and entered her wet hot body, she was so wet and tight it felt like I stuck my shit in a tube of toothpaste with hot butter inside it. When I pushed inside her she opened up her eyes took a deep breath and didn't move I just laid in her for a moment, she got tight around me then I started to move as slow as possible. Cause now anything I do she will get off on. I pushed all the way inside her, she tried to move but I had her pent down. Then I told her that I had been dreaming about this for three years. It worked out with me and Honey that night. Let me say this she calls me DADDY at all times now, and has no problem telling hoes who her man is either.

The next morning Honey got up before me, she had taken her bath and had ordered room service. She had ordered steak and eggs, orange juice and toast. Then I felt a warm rag on my shit, I asked her what she was doing and she said cleaning you up. I have a bath running for you, I said thank you baby she said no thank you baby. Then I fell back a sleep. About thirty minutes or so later I found myself feeling good, breathing hard and had two hands full of sheets. I opened my eyes and all I saw was the covers going up and down, I threw them back and saw Honey looking up at me with a mouth full. It too was hot and wet, bout three minutes later I lost my motherfucking mind. I was trying to get away from her but she had me cornered my head and hands were against the headboard of the bed. I have never bust a nut back to back when I was jacking off. I'm going to be real with you, I didn't know that we could get off like that.

I have asked playas have they ever bust two nuts in a row, and I have always gotten the same answer "no". Honey was a nut cracker when she was finished I told her that I loved her. Then crawled to the bathroom and took a hot bath. While I was in the tub Honey was brushing her teeth. I was watching her ass shake like jelly, I got out the tub and walked in the bedroom butt naked. Honey told me to lay across the bed on my chest, I did. She rubbed lotion all over my whole body, I felt like I was a baby again. I put my clothes on and sat down for breakfast; she cut my steak up for me and had a glass of orange juice ready. She also had the paper for me, shit I felt like I was married. When I got done she Honey pulled out a jay and fired it up, I took a couple of pulls on that piece, I was a cool play boy.

Then Honeys beeper went off, the only person that has the number is Roosevelt. She looked at me, I told her to call Velt and see what's up with him. She called he asked was I with her, she said yeah and passed me the phone. I said hello, Velt said nigga where you at? I told him I was at the hotel, he told me to come to mama's house. I said I'm on my way right now. He said, Lil rose take your time, but come on down we need to talk about something. I told Honey to grab her shit, then we went to big mama's house. When we pulled up there was a lot of cars out, the block was full. I saw Tarzan outside tripping, I parked the car and told Honey to go over there with Candy and Jet. As I was walking up the street I heard Tarzan yelling she's gone Lil rose she's gone, I was like who's gone then I ran into the house. That's where I saw her, big mama was laying on the floor. I asked them why the fuck is everybody just standing around looking, call for some motherfucking help. Pat grabbed me and said they already been here she's gone, then I asked what happened. They said that she had a heart attack, man that fucked me up. I couldn't do nothing but break down and cry, Tarzan came in and grabbed me, Pat and started to cry. Velt told us to go in my room we had other family there, but we were the ones at the house everyday coming and going. People always say I know how you feel, but their mama or daddy is still around walking and talking. But you know how I feel, man if you don't get the fuck outta here with that bullshit. I'll split your mother fucking head bitch. One thing about Tarzan he's gone keep t real with you. I felt him too because in my heart I lost my mother too, and they knew it.

A week passed, were at the same spot three years later my grandmother is put to rest between her husband and first born son. My mother came up from Mississippi, when it was over she came over to big mama's house. Big mama's left the house to her youngest son and that was Pat. We were all at the table when my mama said that we were leaving tomorrow night to go to Mississippi. Roosevelt, Tarzan, Pat, Honey, Candy, and Jet all stopped what they were doing and saying. The dining room got real quite. My mama said did I say something wrong? No one said anything, she said big mama's is gone we gotta look out for Lil rose now. My baby got to come home with me, I had to say something my mama was out of the loop, she was tripping. I said mama I am home, Mississippi doesn't have anything for me. She said Lil rose I know that you don't like it down there, I only have one year of school left. I said that's cool mama I'm proud of you. She said who's gone take care of you now. I said the same people that's been taking care of me when you was in Mississippi. Big mama's gone she said again. I said I lived with big mama off and on. Roosevelt, Tarzan, and Pat been taking care of me here. She said I don't want you living with them, learning about that shit they call the game. I raised you better than that, then I asked her where have you been the past three years of my life. She said boy you know I was in school, I told her me too. I wanted better for you, she said. I told her mama I am a man now, I will take care of myself. She said I just don't want you like them.

Roosevelt said Ann you made that choice a long time ago, when you let him make that trip alone, then you stepped away from his life for three years. Now you back and you want him to step away from his life where he is respected as a man, to go and become your little boy. It's up to him I speak for us up here on his daddy side of the family. We got you Rosewood and my word is bond. My mama said Rosewood who is that? I said that's me, I put my hands to my face.

Then I told Honey to go run me a bath. When she got up Honey said yes daddy and went to the bathroom. My momma just looked at me, she had a crazy look on her face I told my mom she was sleeping in the guest room or she could go to a hotel. She said she was staying. When Honey came back in the room she told me that my bath was done. I told her to go back to the hotel to night, she left I went and took my bath and went to sleep.

The next morning came for my mama to go to the airport. She said I need to call a cab. I told her that I had her, she said baby I miss you. I want you to come back with me to Mississippi. I told her that I have a life here, then I heard Honey outside, I grabbed her bags and took them to the car. My mom said isn't this a eighty nine B.M.W? Honey said yes, my mama said, that when she gets out of school that she wanted to get one. You have a nice car Honey. Honey said thank you but it's not my car, then she walked around the car and opened my driver side door. I told my mama thank you. She said boy that car coast forty thousand dollars. We didn't talk till we got to the airport I hugged her and told her that I loved her. She said after this year is over I will be moving to St. Louis, I told her I would move with her then. I gave her my word as a playa.

CHAPTER SEVEN

Rosewoods Independence

On the way back from the airport the car was quite. Honey was sitting there just looking at me. She said baby everything will be alright. I hope that I didn't hurt her feelings in any way I said. Honey said baby the last time she saw you, you were her baby. Shit your still her baby, she's probably on the plane now tripping off how fast you've grown up. Three years is a long time, she was in school doing her thing to provide for you and your brother. She didn't take the time to trip off you, and you can't fault her for still seeing you as her baby.

I told Honey I feel that and understand your view. Baby, guess what? Honey said what. You are a blessing, I'm going to have to thank Velt for giving me a woman so special. She said no one has ever called me special. I said know why? She said why? Because they don't know what they had on their side. She looked at me and she rubbed me on the side of my face and said, no baby I'm the lucky one cause to me your special. No one ever took the time to know me and cared about how I felt about things, all they wanted me to do is be cute. Do what they say and open my legs when the wind blew. I said don't get me wrong now, I'm looking for the same thing. I started laughing and she said fuck you nigga and pushed me in the head. Then I said hold up bitch, keep your hands off this pimping. She said yes daddy.

I had to get back into playa mode. I have learned over the years, a true playa must show off their softer side every once in a while. That keeps his females feeling needed and she will stay in pocket. In pocket means, to stay in your corner through thick and thin. If you are real smooth with it, she would be willing to do a hundred and fifty years for you. I pulled up on my home boy from school and said, what's up sunny boy? He said my niggga Lil rose what's going on with you? Nothing I told him my new name was Rosewood now, he just looked at me. He said there's a nigga out here named Rosewood, you ain't heard he set it off at the last playas ball. I said nigga my name is Rosewood. He said alright man, who's car s this it's clean. Its mine pimping I said. Yours, man get the fuck outta here he said. I got tired of fucking with this dumb ass nigga. I told Sunny boy to met me at the barber shop around five o'clock. He said okay then I mashed out.

I told Honey that I was going to drop her off at Roosevelt's house for a few hours, she said that she was cool with that. When I got to Velt's house, he was in the backyard by the pool. I pulled up on him he was wearing blue silk pj's with some blue gaiters on, the water in the pool was an ocean blue. Man that nigga was looking way O.G in the game. Candy and Jet was on both sides of him in blue two piece swim suite the sight looked gangsta. I said what's up pimping Rose? He said same soup just trying to reheat it. Hopefully I can find a pretty young bitch that's down with this pimping. Then he asked what's up with you Rosewood?

I said slow motion like the ocean, just sitting back staying focus thinking about ways I can pimp the nation. I can feel that Rosewood, and honor that thought Velt said. Did your mama leave this morning? I said yeah, I asked him did I handle that at the table last night. He said yeah because in her eyes you are still her baby. You just had to let her know that you had a voice now. The last time she saw you, you didn't have a voice, and she will be alright. I said you think so, he said man I know your mama she's stronger than that trust me.

I asked him what was he doing up at seven thirty in the morning. He said this is the best time to think about life. The world is quite right now. The world I live in has just went to sleep. So this is the best time to move while the playas are sleep, because when they are up they can trip off my moves in the game. You can't trip off of what you can't see in this game. This is the time when the streets Ain't watching or talking. I couldn't say nothing Velt just dropped a seed. That was very important information to a playa in the game. That's playing for keeps, then he asked me to stay for a minute. I said okay then he called Candy outside. When she came out she was looking at me crazy. I already knew what she was tripping on, I know honey told them about what went down in the hotel. Shit that's what they are taking about in the kitchen now. Velt told her to go get the chess board and bring us some refer and some hen. This time the only thing I said was hi. When she walked away she looked me up and down and smiled. I never have seen that kind of smile come from her before. This one here was freaky, when she walked away she was shaking that ass. See Candy know she is a bad motherfucker. One day I asked her, why they call you Candy. She said, have you ever had a box of candy that was so good when you got to the last piece you wish you had some more. I said yeah, she said now look at me. I couldn't do nothing but smile. As Velt and I sat there he said, I see you didn't ask her to get anything for you. I said last time I was in the wrong. A playa must stay in character at all times pimping. He said Lil rose you learn fast. I said uncle Roosevelt I don't mean no disrespect, but my name is Rosewood now. He said, I can't do nothing but respect that. You are a man now and the game respects you as Rosewood. I'm proud of you pimp, I also know that if your father were here he would say the same thing. He would probably be mad at me for letting you grow up so fast, I said you know he would pimping. We both started laughing.

Candy came back out and Honey was with her. I tried to bring it right out, but Honey said that I wasn't going to bring her man shit. Honey had my drink and my weed on my own tray. Jet called Velt on the phone, then Candy and Velt went back in the house. I told Honey thank you for what she did. She said it was nothing, I told her she was wrong it means the world to me. She was smiling from ear to ear, I told her to come sit on daddy's lap. She came over and sat down, I put my arm around her waist and asked her did she trust me? She said, yeah baby why did you ask me that, I said baby it's about you and me now.

Do you know I didn't leave with my mama? Yeah because you didn't want to live in Mississippi, she said. I told her that wasn't the reason it was you I don't want to lose you. She just looked at me, she didn't say a word. Then I said, baby in the life that I'm in I mean that were in we must keep our business just with us. Because it's us against the world, and our world is about sex, money, and murder. Do you feel where I'm at on this, she said yeah baby I understand. Then I told her to go pack her things and call me if she needed help putting it in the car. She asked where are we going, I told her that we were going to stay at big mama's house. Honey said okay and kissed me on the cheek. By this time Candy and Velt were coming back out to the pool. Honey started walking off I hit her on the butt and said that's my girl.

Velt pulled back up to the table, and said sorry that took so long on the phone pimping. I told him that it was cool pimping, I asked him, do you mind if Honey moved with me to big momma's house? He said listen Rosewood that's your woman now I don't care what you do with her. Do you want me to tell her she has to kick rocks? I said no pimping I already told her to pack her things. But I do need you to let her keep her job till I beat you five times on the chess board. Then I can get my own money in the game, and stand on my own two feet as a man. He looked at me and said, I got you nephew and I'm going to give her twenty-five hundred every two weeks. I want you to stack some money, so when you break out and choose you hustle your paper will be right. I said, thanks man I am blessed to have a nigga like you in my corner, because you look out for me like my old dude did. He said, boy I love you and I would fuck something up about you. I said, I feel the same way about him. He said he knew. I laid back in my lawn chair, fired up a fat bat, and took a sip of hen straight. After about ten minutes, Velt started to break the game of chess down to me. He said that this is the game of life and every piece is a hustler in the game we play in the street. This is the King, he is the most important piece in the game, this is you. In the game in the streets everyone is a King. They will only think about protecting their own ass. When someone fucks with you on any level in life, it's all about what they use you for. It's all about them, so when you fuck with them your goal is to find out what they want and how to put security on yourself. Cause it's all about you in this game. This is the Queen. This is the next piece that is important to the King. The Queen in the game is your right hand, it could be your woman or home boy. I have found out over the years that a woman is more loyal than a man in the game. But you have to treat her right. You can treat a nigga right and it's still not enough, because he wants to be on top. It's up to you to let the Queen know what to do. But at the same time you have to watch the Queens moves to, cause she can get you fucked up in the game. Have you heard the saying "don't let your right hand know what your left hand is doing." I said, yeah then he said, that goes with the queen in the game.

These two pieces here are the bishops. The bishops are them niggas that you call from out of town to cause a problem and take niggas out the way. You can afford to lose them, the sweet thing about them is niggas can't tie them to you. Keep them out of sight you never know who they might get in the game. These here are the knights, they are the two that come through and fuck shit up. When niggas see them they know that you want them to feel your presence in the game, and it's like and there is no rapping it's all business. These two are your rooks, they are your personal body guards. They always move with you, when people see you they see them.

Last these are your street niggas, the pawns. There job is to press the game on the street level. Did you understand all that? I said, yeah. Well run it back down to me then he said. I said, well I see it like a corporation. The King is the president, the Queen is the vice president, the bishops and knights are head of security, the rooks are security, and the pawns are the workers. How's that? He said, boy you are a mother, you're quick on your feet that's a beautiful thing.

Then I heard Honey call me to help her put her stuff in the car. Roosevelt told Candy and Jet help her. Then he showed me the way each piece moved, now that was a mother fucker there. That took me a while to learn and move comfortable. I played a couple of games before I had to roll out. I still had some business to take care of today.

We talked for a minute and then he said ah yeah before I forget that was that nigga Moon from Miami calling to talk to you. I told him you were out of town for a few weeks, I told him you were looking forward to talking to him. I asked Roosevelt what was up with him? Velt said that moon has been in the game for a long time. He started young when he got his feet wet. He is three hundred and sixty five degrees in the game, even the police respect him. I asked him what was his secret? He told me it was all about respect in the game of life.

If he likes you he will put you on top of the game, his hands are like all state baby boy. He is also good people, when you are ready you need to make your way down there pimping. I told Velt I had to make a move and I would see him later on in the game. I made it back to the car, when we jumped back on the express way honey asked me a question. She said, baby why did you ask me by the pool? I said, because when candy came outside where we was she was looking at me all crazy. Then when our eyes met she lick her lips, so I figured you had to be in there talking about us. She said, baby you know what? I said, what. I was talking about us and you caught that just by looking at her body movements. I pulled up in the drive way at big mama's house. When I opened the door the house felt so cold, it was dark and quiet it just didn't feel like home anymore. I went and grab Honey's things out of the car, I told her to fix up the guess room cause it was the bigger one and had the Queen size bed. I asked her was she cool by herself for a while?

She said that she was cool, she had a lot to do to get it to feel like home for both of us. I said, okay then headed out on my mission. I pulled up at the barber shop about five forty five, Sunny boy was in the shop getting a haircut. I walked in and pimp Sue was talking about the playas ball. When he saw me he said, what's up Mr. Rosewood. I said slow mother fucking motion like the ocean I'm trying to find a way to rape the nation. Pimp Sue can you feel that? He said, from my head to my toes you find out how, and then get at me pimping. I said foe show toe tapper.

After what went down at the ball I need to be calling you toe tapper, he said. I said, don't start that Sue keep that under your hat pimping. He started to laugh and said, ok I got you on the underbelly. He asked me did the playa of the year get at me? I told him that I talked to Moon about an hour ago. I know and you know, but he didn't. Anyway Pimp Sue know that the streets is watching me right now real close. Buy him saying that he know the streets is listening too. So now they know that the top playa in the bubble right now wants me on his team. I told pimp sue nice looking out. He said, out of respect for another playa in the game. Right then I knew he wanted to get money with me on any level I would let him in on. I said, we are gone get down like four flat tires then I tipped my hat to him. He said then there was, I said some more of it pimping. The rest of the shop was just looking, they were trying to put the conversation together but they couldn't. It was to gangsta for radio.

Then Sunny boy was done getting his hair cut. He asked me what's up? I told him lets go to the rim store. He said for what, I told him that I was getting some rims for the B.M.W. Nigga I thought you was bull shitting home boy, he said. I know you did that's why I wanted you to meet me so we could talk about some business. What kind of business? He said. Now you got business, I said nigga I'm gone to holla at you about it. But if you keep talking that shit, I'm going to let your dusty ass keep asking your mama for money little ass nigga. Fuck it nigga I'm cool on you, I jumped in the B.M.W and went to the rim shop.

I meet a hustle ass nigga named Everyday, they call him that because every time you saw him he had something to sell a nigga. If he didn't have it give him a couple of days and he had it. He was in the shop getting some rims on his eighty seven I-Roc Z twenty eight with tee tops in it. His car was black with tan interior, he told me that he was getting some chrome I-Roc rims. I pulled up in there, after I told the dude what I was looking for. I said, Everyday what's up playa. He said what's up Lil Rose? I told him that my name was Rosewood now. He said shit that's you, I said yeah why what's up. He said, I heard what went down at the playas ball my baby mama's uncle was there.

When they came home that was all they could talk about was how you set it off for Detroit. Since then I have been asking motherfuckers all over the city about who was Rosewood. Shit and I already know who you are, man it's a small world play boy. I said, that it is playa, then he asked me who's car was that? Mine I said, then he asked me what year it was. I said, it a eighty nine. How much is the note? He asked. That's paid for playa, I said. He asked what rims where I going to put on it. I said that I was getting some old Dayton wire wheels with thin black walls. He said shit that motherfucker there gone be a bad boy, you gone crush these niggas here. I said, that's the plan. Midnight blue with tan interior on all good ones, Rosewood that's pimping there play boy. I'm going to wait to see that, I'm not going anywhere till they pull that peace out, he said. I said, that's cool because I wanted to talk to you about some business.

The dude told me that the rims cost twenty eight hundred. I still had the money that Honey gave me. When Everyday seen that knot he said, Rosewood I'm ready to get that paper playa. I told him to give me his beeper number when I'm ready I will tell him the play. Then they pulled out my car out. I must say that it was so pretty, I jumped in it and went to the car phone store and bought one. That took a half hour, I called home and Honey picked up the phone and said hello. I said what's up baby. She said hi daddy. I asked her if she wanted me to pick anything up before I come home. She said, yeah get some strawberries and whip cream. I said okay and I hung up the phone. I went through the carwash real fast hit the store and went home.

When I came in the house was dark, I made my way to the dining room where I saw candles lit on the table. There was dinner on the table for two, I saw Honey sitting in the chair with a white teddy on with her legs crossed, and she had on white pumps too. She said, welcome home baby. I said, let me go put this in kitchen she said sit down I will put that stuff up in the kitchen, she grabbed the bag from me. Then she walked away. I told her that I hate to see her go, but love to watch you walk away. She smiled and started walking so nasty. I found myself biting on my bottom lip. I sat down at the table and tripped off how she set the table. She made steak and potatoes, red wine and fresh baked bread. She even had some weed rolled for me. When she came back to the table she picked up my knife and fork then cut my steak up for me. I looked in her eyes and told her that she was so beautiful and I was lucky to have her in my life.

She then she kissed on my cheek. She whispered in my ear baby go ahead and eat before it gets cold. The whole time I was eating she was drinking and just looking at me from across the table. I could feel her foot under the table moving between my legs. Then she looked at me with bedroom eyes as she rubbed her finger around the top of the glass. I saw it in her eyes she wanted to get down like she lived. The light from the candles was real soft and she had her hair down. All I saw in her was the Cubin side. I wanted to know what she was thinking, so I asked her. Honey, she said real soft yeah baby. I said what's on your mind baby? You she said. I started smiling, I was through eating. She got up and got my plate and took it to the kitchen. When she came back she had the strawberries and a bucket of ice, with the whip cream. She told me to slide my chair back from the table, I did then she lit up a bat and gave it to me. I started smoking it, Honey stood there and started taking off her teddy. She pulled down her top her breast was fat and beautiful. Then she went in the front room and got a pillow off the couch, and laid it on the floor in front of me. She told me to stand up, I did she unbuttoned my pants and told me to step out of them.

Then she went in the bedroom, when she came back with a hanger and a towel in her hand. She hung my pants up then gave me the towel. Then she put a strawberry in my wine.

Then I tried to give her some weed she said that she was cool. Then she said sit down, I did. Now that weed and drink was doing their thing, I closed my eyes and lean my head back and blew out that reefer. Honey put ice in her mouth and started sucking on my nuts. I stood right up. Then I felt something warm and wet, I looked down she was looking up at me, and moved slowly up and down again and again over and over. She closed her eyes and started licking on me like tootsie roll pop. Then she popped a strawberry in her mouth and opened her eyes and looked at me, then she got back down like she lived. I was still smoking on that bat, she stood up and took her teddy all the way off.

I put everything down, she stood up over me and got on top. She was still chewing on the strawberry but now she was looking down at me and we were eye to eye. I tried to grab my shit, she told me to grab her ass tight and she will do everything else. I started kissing on her dark brown nipples and licking on her big brown breast. She took her hand and grabbed my shit and then she slid down on to me. It was tight hot and wet. She put her hands around my head and started to bounce up and down. she, had a nice slow beat like boom, boom, boom, boom, boom, boom, boom, boom, boom, boom. At the same time she was speaking Spanish, the only thing I could understand was papi. I knew she was about to cum because the beat was getting faster and faster. She was getting louder too and she moved her hands up under my arm pits, to get some grip and she started to bounce harder and harder. She called my name she said oh my God Rosewoooooood and she got super wet.

I felt cum dripping down between my legs and off my nuts. Then she stood up and turned around and opened her legs then bent over the table and she rubbed her hand in her stuff and got her hand super wet. Then rubbed her hand in the crack of her butt, then she grabbed my shit and slid it in her butt. It was super tight and wet I almost didn't get in. When I entered her, I heard her grown and I put my hands around her hips and went wild like a cave man. She was looking back at me and I could see pain in her face. Then I lost my mind when I came in her.

CHAPTER EIGHT

Play Time Is Over

Two months had passed, the summer is over I am in the tenth grade now. As for the summer I can say I made a name for myself on the streets. My chess game has stepped all the way up. I be giving Uncle Roosevelt the blues now. A couple of nights ago I bet him four times. On the fifth game he took so long to move, he made me make a mistake and gave him the game. I got a plan now, I know what to do the next time we play. I know you want to know what's up with Honey and me. Were in the game together like a ball and glove playa. We have learned how each other move over the past few months. I must say it's been a beautiful thing. Me and that nigga Everyday has been getting a little paper off and on. I did it that way so we can learn how we move in the game together. One thing I can say about Everyday he's a hustling ass nigga.

I have two weeks before my birthday, my goal to is to beat uncle Roosevelt on that chess shit. I believe it's time for me to get my feet wet in the game. A week then passed, I'm up on Velt in the chess war, the count is four. Before he could drag the game through the mud I told him I had something to do, then I left. He tried to one two me, but I was up on that nigga. When I got in the car I had to call Honey. Hello, what's up baby? She said, that Pat was back in town and he wanted me to call him. I said ok. I asked her did she want something before I came home, she said that she was cool. Then she said, bring yo fine ass home. I told her, that I was going to call pat baby be careful and that she loved me. I said, back to her. I called pat. What's up nigga He said what's up with you Rosewood. I said that I was trying to shake the street down with Everyday. Pat started laughing and said that Everyday fucks him up. I said Everyday is about paper Pat. He said I feel you. I said you can't feel us, because you won't let me hold no weight so I can get some of that real paper out here. He said, shit man Roosevelt made me give my word that I wouldn't give you nothing till you beat him at chess. By the way what's the count now, I said it's four zero my way.

Tomorrow I will go finish him off. He said, if you win tell Velt to call me and I will have something special for you. That's music to my ears right there, I said. Then he asked me where was I calling from? I said the car, I hear you playa he said. Hey I'm moving back in a couple of month's, do you think that enough time for you and Honey to find a spot. I said, your coming to get the house. He said damn right I Ain't putting you out but my girl is coming with me. I know two hoes living in the same house Ain't gone work out. But if your money Ain't right you can stay and Honey can go back out there to Velts. I said, pimping that Ain't going down, we cool you can come get the spot now. He said hold up Rosewood I Ain't like that at all, I said I know it Ain't Pat. But that is the only place I know to call home man. That's the last thing I have of my daddy and big Mama, but I know it's yours now I can't do nothing but respect your wishes play boy. I will start looking for something tomorrow. He said take your time baby boy. Alright Pat I will get back at you tomorrow I said. Ok he said, then I called Honey back and told her to run me a real hot bath and to put some bubbles in it. She said, ok. Then I stopped at the store and ran into pimp Sue. What's poppin pimp Sue. He said, shit I just got back from Iowa. Iowa I said, he said yeah I been looking for a spot to put the rape down, and I think I found it. I asked him how long was he going be in town? He said a few days. I told him to give a number so I could get in contact with him in the next couple of days. He gave me a couple of numbers, I shook his hand and tipped my hat to him got my shit and mashed out to the crib.

When I got home Honey met me in the front room, she had my robe and house shoes ready for me. She told me that she heard stress in my voice over the phone. My bath was ready and had bubbles in it like I asked. When I was at the store I picked up a long steamed white rose for her and some rolling paper and a bottle of crown royal. When I got in the tub it was so hot it took about a half hour to sit all the way down in the water. When I did it felt so good, I couldn't do nothing but close my eyes and lay my head back and just soaked my body.

Fucking with the streets will stress you out, I think its cause you're dealing with cut throat ass niggas and game runners. But when you make it home to the war room, everything must be just right. Because it is the place where you get your mind together. So when you go back out in the streets your mind is clear, you must have a mission when you leave the house. Cause when you don't anything can happen to you, your just out in the world with no goals. You might end up anywhere or with anybody. Honey came in the bathroom and sat by the tub, she had a drink and a jay for me. Then she asked, what's on your mind? I opened my eyes and just looked at her then she asked why was I looking at her like that? I said I was thinking about how lucky I am, I'm also tripping off how beautiful you are. I asked her to come closer to the tub then I kissed her on the cheek. When she sat back down on the floor she was smiling. Then she asked what was up with Pat?

I told her, she said that Ain't nothing but a thing there. We could move tomorrow if you wanted to. I said, baby I know I told that nigga that myself. Let's not talk about that right now ok. She said ok. Then I told her tomorrow we need to start looking around for something nice. She said a house or an apartment? I told her an apartment, its only me and you. She said I hope to change that one day. I asked her what are you trying to say, she said Rose one day not now. I said one day we could make that happen. Then she got behind me and started washing my back and rubbing my shoulders and chest.

I got up the next morning around six o'clock. I was getting ready for school and for some reason I felt like a real playa today. I put on some dark blue 100% cotton slacks, a pair of blue gaiters and a navy blue silk short sleeved shirt. My waves were busting, they were thick deep and waved the fuck up. My beard was trimmed neat and lined up. I had my nails done and buffed out, I had a pair of diamond earrings a gold watch and bracelet on. I also had on a gold pinky ring with diamonds in it, that was my old dudes ring.

And last but not least Velt let me have his chain, a gold rope with a lions head on it with two diamond eyes in it. I must say that I was clean as a mother fucker on the first day of school. When I pulled up in front of the school, Everyday and a couple of his homeboys were out front. All three of them were rolling I-Rocs with tee tops in them. The front of the school was packed with a gang of people looking and talking about what people were driving and wearing. When I pulled up all eyes were on me, the B.M.W was clean and them all gold Dayton's set it off. I pulled up with the driver's side facing the school. I sat there Honey got out of the car and walked around to the driver's side, I saw all the guy's with their mouths open checking Honey out. Then she opened my door and I stepped out the car. Honey gave me a knot and kissed me on the cheek, when she got in the car I closed the door.

I told her to wait till I gave her the sign before she left. She asked when do you want me to pick you up? I told her around two fifteen she said ok. Then I walked away from the car towards the school. I heard Everyday say rosewood over here man, I went over there with Everyday and his crew. Everyday said playa I see you putting your thing down pimping. Hey this is my home boy Slow and this right here is Jap. This man right here is Rosewood, I said what's up to both of them. Then I turned around and blew a kiss to Honey and she blew one back, then pulled off. I saw Sunny boy just looking at me, I told him to come here. When he came over I told him long time no see play boy. He said, why you stop fucking with a nigga Rosewood? I said, Sunny boy I came to you on some business, and you kept coming to me on some bullshit like I was a little boy or something.

Shit nigga I got true playas from all over the bubble that want me on their team, and they respect me. You was my friend, but you couldn't respect me as a man. So I stopped fucking with you all together. See lil nigga it all about paper in the real world, I'm on that big boy shit I'm in the streets now. At the barber shop you showed me then that you were still in school. I tripped off you all day. But then it came to me, the school yard might be the best place for you. He said, man I was playing, I said yeah you played yourself. Man let me get in where I fit in then, he said. I said Sunny boy let me think about it, I will get back at you later on that, when I need you. He said, bet Mr. Rosewood. I will holla at you pimping.

It's now twelve thirty, lunch time. I made my way down to the lunch room when I walked past a white woman standing at the teachers lunch room door. She was just looking at me up and down. I felt like she was undressing me with her eyes. I must say she was a bad white girl. She was about five-nine slim with long sexy legs. She had dark blonde hair with deep blue eyes, She also had a nice tan. She must have some paper, because in Detroit white people have pale skin cause its cold most of the year. She also had on black framed glasses and a tight blue sweater; if I had to take a guess I would say she is a D or C cup in her breast size. She had a nice tight butt with a little tight mouth. Shit if I get a chance I would jack my mack on that hoe. But right now is to early in the game to say anything but hi to her now. I need more information on her, she was new to I didn't see her last year.

So when I walked past her I stopped and said hello, then asked her how to get to the lunch room. She smiled and took a step backwards and told me were the lunch room was. I told her that I was sorry for walking up on her that close, then told her that I was new and was kind of shy to ask a beautiful woman like herself where the lunch room was. She ate that bullshit right up and looked like she wanted some more of it. She said, don't worry about it I'm new too. I told her thank you and walked off. When I hit the steps I looked up in the bubble mirror on the corner of the stairs, she was still watching me when I hit the corner.

When I made it to the lunch room people were all over the place. They was sectioned off in groups, I heard everybody calling me. A nigga was yelling my name loud as a motherfucker. Put it like this if you didn't know my name you did now. When I made my way through the lunch room all eyes were on me, that was cool though. When everyone does that, that means that there interested in what they see. Now at the same time niggas that want it like that for themselves. Two things are going to happen, one is that they are going to find a way in your group. That's playa, and two is they are going to try to find something wrong with you. So you must be careful on the way you move and dress, cause the streets is watching your moves on every level of the game.

I finely made it over to Everyday and his crew, these niggas are the shit at school. They are young and getting that paper. This is their last year in school, so you know how that goes. All the little girls want to be there girlfriends. So they can look down on the rest of the school like they are the shit. Everyday asked me what I was doing after school today. I told him I had some business to take care of. He said, on that money? I asked, what else is it? He said, nothing and we both smiled. Jap and Slow was just looking at me, I asked them how were they getting down on that paper? They both answered on the corner, they asked me how was I getting mine. I said, play boys I get mine three hundred and sixty-five ways. And at the end of the day my knot be so fat I could choke a horse, you know how fat a horse neck is. Jap said that I was bullshitting, then Everyday said lay on back play boy that nigga is straight up with that shit. We have been getting paper over the summer. This nigga is a true playa. I told Everyday, I was up to my next class play boy, then, I left.

My first day of school was over when I went outside Honey was right there waiting for me standing against the car with a yellow rose in her hand. When I was walking down the steps I saw the teacher, I asked her how was her first day? She smiled and said ok. Then she asked me did I meet any new friends today. I smiled and said, yeah if I can call you my friend. She smiled again and said, yeah you can call me your friend. I told her I was going to hold her to that, she said ok. Don't let me hold you up I don't want you to miss your bus. I told her that I don't catch the bus I drive to school, my ride is right there. She said where, I didn't say anything I just walked off towards Honey. I asked Honey was that for me?

She said yeah, then she hugged me and gave me a kiss. I said what was that for? I missed you, she said then opened the door for me. When I got in the car the air was bumping, it was hot outside too. This morning it was cool out. She closed the door and walked around the front of the car. I looked up at the steps and the teacher was still there looking at me. I picked up the phone and called Velt and told him to get the board ready, and that it's going down today. I am going to win my independents today. He said young nigga I been thinking about whipping yo ass all night. I said bet I'm on my way pop's, he laughed then I pulled off.

On my way to Velts house Honey asked how was my day at school. I said everything was cool today. Then it came, she asked me who was that I was talking to on the steps. I said, Honey the first thing I'm going to tell you is don't worry about my business if I don't ask you anything about time. Do you under stand me? She looked away from me and said, ok. What the fuck is ok? It's a yes or no question. She looked back at me and said that she understood. Then I told her that the woman I was talking to was a new teacher. Then I asked her why did she ask any way?

She looked away again and said that she saw how she was looking at you. Then I asked her what did she see? She looked back at me and said, I saw that she liked what she saw. When you were talking to her. She couldn't stop laughing at your jokes. Baby I know ho's out here want you and I'm going to have to deal with that. I'm not a little girl, but I really love you. Then I see ho's all up in your face I get hot.

Then I said baby you know the game we play is a dirty one. You know that I must play on the lames feelings to get our paper up. Then she said I know baby, you have to understand that I have never loved anyone before.

Baby it's nothing next time just check your feelings at the door when you leave the house. She laughed and said ok. Then I told her whatever I do in the streets when I come home to her I will leave it in the streets. You are my world and only you. She dropped her head and I saw her beautiful smile. For the next ten minutes it was quite in the car. Honey was looking out the window thinking to herself, I was driving thinking to myself about the chess game I was going to play with Velt. I was also thinking about getting another car, because I can see where this shit is heading already and it's only the first day of school. I need to knock this shit in the head as quick as possible, as I pulled into Velts driveway I grabbed Honey's hand and told her to stay right here. Then I got out of the car with the rose she bought me. When I started walking around the car I saw Candy and Jet in the door looking, I opened the door for her, and grabbed her hand as she stepped out the car. I gave her the rose and kissed her on the cheek.

We walked in the door hand in hand she had a smile on her face so big. I found out later in the game that a man has never held her hand and walked somewhere with her. So that move right there blew her mind. Something that is nothing to one person means the world to another. When we walked through the door Candy and Jet was looking crazy, I asked Candy where was Velt. I heard his voice in the living room say, I'm in here Rosewood. Jet said damn Rosewood you don't speak to a bitch no more. I said, baby you know I got love for your beautiful black ass. I told her to give me a hug. I walked in the living room with Velt, the board was already set up and he had made his first move. When I sat down Candy was already coming with the drinks then she said she would be back with the joints. I grabbed my drink and said thank you, and made my move. About ten minutes passed then Candy came back in the room, she had changed clothes. She had on some red hills, some red guarders on her legs that snapped to her red G-string that was all in her ass. And she had on a red top that was lose and had it tied in a knot between her breast, she didn't have a bra on either. She had the weed Velt told me to fire it up, I told him that I was cool. He looked at me then told

Candy can she light it up and give him a shot gun. She lit it up then turned her back to me. She threw her leg over his knee, then sat on it. I must say she had a beautiful ass. I told Velt that it was his move.

She turned back around towards me on his knee, then he made his move. I was putting the press down slowly but surely. I trapped his Queen and took it with a knight. He was mad as a motherfucker now without his queen that fucks his game all the way up. I know that he feels me now, he told Candy to light up another joint up. Then he took both of my rooks to push his king to the middle of the board. Then my knights started killing everything around him. I saw him hit Candy on the butt, she opened her legs wide open and kept them that way. I saw what was going on, she was sent in here to fuck with me. That's why she was doing all the shit she was doing.

He asked me why I wasn't drinking with him. I said I meant no disrespect but I was so in the game I forgot about it. I picked it up and played like I was knocking it off, then I asked him if I could hit the joint. He passed it to me, I only need three moves to check mate his ass. I know that he is going to take all day now to make me hot and started fucking up. But not this time, I called honey in the front room. I told her to go out to the car and get that blunt I had in the glove box. When she came back in I told her to give me the weed. I asked Velt did he have a razor blade, he said yeah and told Jet to bring it to me. I told Honey to go to the kitchen and get some honey.

When she came back he asked me what the fuck you doing boy. I told him it was his move. I took the razor and cut the blunt down the middle. He moved and I moved, now I only need two moves. I dumped all the guts out of the blunt, then took the honey from Honey and put it on the inside of the blunt. It was just enough to cover the paper then I put a lot of weed in it. Velt said what are you doing with that weed, you just fucked it up. I told him that's my shit pimping it your move. He looked at me crazy and went back to the game.

I rolled it up nice and tight, then put more honey on the outside of it. Then I asked Honey to put it on the air conditioner vent. He moved I moved. Now I need one more move to win my independents in the game. I told Honey that it should be cool by now, she brought it back to me asked Roosevelt if he had a light. He said he didn't have one, Candy said she had it in her hand. Velt said, bitch give him a light then and leave me the fuck alone, I'm trying to think right now. It's working I'm getting to him. I fired that cold motherfucker up and took a long ass drag. I started coughing I heard Honey say that it don't smell like weed it smell like cookies. It was burning slow too. Every time I blew I blew the smoke in Velt face on the slide. I know he was tripping off of it because of the way he was looking up from time to time. Then I did it again, he looked back up and said, why are you blowing that shit up in my face playa. Candy, Jet, and Honey was just looking at us. I moved up to the edge of my chair and looked at Velt then said it's your move, and to come on cause, I had some business to handle.

Then I blew smoke up in the air sat back in my chair and crossed my legs. I told Honey to come and stand beside her daddy. She came over and stood beside her man, he moved then looked at me. He was so use to me moving right behind him, he looked at me I looked at him then he looked at the board. I heard Candy say what do you call that your smoking, I said a honey blunt after my baby. Velt snapped his fingers Candy and Jet stopped talking and went to both sides of his chair. Velt saw it, he sat back in the chair and crossed his legs. I made my last move, then I sat back and crossed my legs and said check mate pimping. I was free in the game.

Chapter Nine

Now It's My Time

As we sat in the chairs just looking at each other, the room was quite. I was smoking on a honey blunt with Honey standing my beside me with her hand on my shoulder. Velt was sitting there with his legs crossed with Candy and Jet standing on each side of him of his chair. Velt looked at me and said, so Rosewood how do you want to get down in the game? Well first I need you to call Pat to get that block up off me. Second I need a loan of ten thousand dollars. Third I would like you to be a middle man between Moon and myself. Forth I would like to know if Honey could still work for you just on drop off for a little while longer? my last request is to give you a huge and I would like to tell you thank you and that I love you for everything.

He set there and told me that all my request will be done. Then he told Candy to go get that money. She took her sexy self right on up stairs. Then he told Jet to go get the phone and to call Pat right now, then she took off. Then he asked me if he could hit that honey blunt? I said yeah, then I give it to Honey and she took it to him. Then she walked right back to me and took her place standing right beside me. Candy came back in the room with the money. Jet walked in right behind her with the phone. She gave the phone to Velt. He said hello Pat the block is off. Yeah he beat me. I threw all the tricks in the game at him.

Like I said all the tricks at him, I had Honey tripping with him when she picked him up. I tried to get him high and drunk. I even pulled the Candy card and he wasn't fucking with nothing. Shit to be real with you he got me off into my feelings. He's ready now, well bless him man. You know June blessed you when it was your time. Alright I'll tell him, peace play boy. Then he gave the phone back to Jet and she walked back out of the room. Candy gave him the money. It was a thousand dollars a wrap. He dropped ten wraps on me. I couldn't do nothing but smile. Then I told him that it was time for me to leave. He told me that he understand, and stood up too walk me to the door. When I made it to the door I turned around and said, you still haven't done one of my request. Then he asked me which one was it? Then I gave him a huge and told him that I loved him. Then I took my first step out of his house right in to the game.

It was about six o'clock now, we jumped in the car and pulled off. The first thing I did was picked up the phone and called Pat. When he picked up I said, what's up man I'm on my way over. He laughed and said I knew you was. I told him to give me about thirty minutes. He told me ok playa I'll be here. Then I huge up the phone. Then I asked Honey why didn't she tell me what Velt had up his sleeve? She said that we had to see how you handle yourself when you have a lot of shit on your mind. That's all don't look at me like that Rose. I wouldn't done that if it wasn't Velt, I saw the good in it.

I didn't say anything I was just looking straight ahead driving. Then she asked me what was I thinking about? I still didn't say anything, I pick up the phone and called the cab company and gave them Pat's address. Five minutes later I pulled up to Pat's crib. I told Honey to stay in the car then I got out and walked into Pat's house with her pocket book. Pat met me at the door. When I walked in he said what's up play boy? Then he asked me who was in the car? I told him that was Honey in the car. Why didn't you tell her to come in? I told him that she will in a couple of minutes. Then I asked him what did he have for me? Then he pushed a bag on me and said that this was from Tarzan and myself. When I looked off in the bag it was a brick of dope. Then I asked him what did he mine. He told me that all this was for me to paper up with. Then he asked me did I have someone to get it hard. I told him that I had some one in mind. I walked back to the door and called Honey in. when she came in I gave her the bag and told her that I need her to drop it off. She saw what I had and said ok. Then we heard a horn blow out side. When Pat looked out of the window he was a cab in his driveway.

Honey grab her pocket book and give me a kiss. Then she walked out of the door and jumped into the cab. I told pat that I would caught up with him later. I waited until the cab pulled off then I want outside and jumped into my car and followed the cab home. On the way home I called Everyday and told him to meet at the barber shop in about an hour. He said ok, then we pulled up at the house. Honey was at the door waiting on me to open it. Once we made it in the house. She said that she got the cab driver's number and he said that he will take us anywhere in the city. All yeah it's all off the record. I kissed her on the cheek and told her good job. Then I told her to put that brick on the table. To the one's who don't know what a brick is it's a kilo of cocaine. Pat had every oz was in it's own bag. So I had thirty six oz of soft in a bag. I grab four of them and put the rest up in the wall. Then I told Honey to call that cab back for me. I told her that I was going back to the shop I will be back later on. Then I heard the cab outside. I jumped in and told him my name and where to go and we pulled off. Then I asked him what was his name, he told me white boy. I couldn't do nothing but smile. Then I told him that I would give him a hundred dollars every time I use him. He said that's a hundred a day when you use me, White boy said that's cool. Then he said that he don't know nothing and will not ask any question. I had to tell white boy that I could respect that. Then I tapped him on his shoulder and gave him a hundred dollar bill.

We pulled up to the shop, I told White boy to wait on me. Then I jumped out of the cab and walked into the shop. When I walked in I saw pimp sue was there. I pulled up on him in the chair and told him that I will talk to him before I leave and I was cool. He shook his head up and down and smiled. I moved over to Everyday and told him I had something I needed to get hard. He told me to come on let's roll. I told him to pull in front the cab. As I walked towards the door I told Pimp sue that I would talk to him later. When I walked outside I told Everyday that I was going to follow him to the honey cone hide out. Pimp sue comes to the door, I asked him when was he going back to Iowa? He said tomorrow, I told him that I was coming to Iowa in a couple of weeks. So he should get everything in order. He smiled and said that he would call me in two weeks and point me in the right way. I said cool then he walked back into the shop. When we pulled in front of the honey cone hide out. I told white boy to go back on duty. I will call you later on. He told me alright then pulled off. When I walked in I saw Jap and Slow in the kitchen sitting at the table. I asked them who knew that magic on that work. Slow stood up and said Rosewood I know how to bubble that soft to hard. I smiled and said well let's get that lab together then play boy. Then he asked me how much was we cooking? I told him right now it four oz. Then he told me that he could turn that four into eight. I turned back around and said get the fuck out of here. Slow told Jap to get some seven up from the store. Jap said ok as he walked out of the door.

Slowly started pulling shit from everywhere. I saw baking soda and some shit called b-12. Then he had a big ass pickle jar in the sink. Jap was back within minutes from the store with the seven up in hand. Slow put a little water in the bottom of the pickle jar. Then he put the baking soda in with the dope. Behind that was the b-12 then he put a lot of seven up in the jar. He kept moving the jar around the fire so that the dope wouldn't stick to the side of the jar. While slow was doing his thing I told Jap and everyday to come up front so we could talk. When we all set down I asked Everyday if his girl was getting food stamp? He told me that she was. Then I told him to have her sign up for section eight or low income housing and you move to the projects. Everyday looked at me and said that me and my girl stayed with my mom. I don't want my little girl to be raised in the projects. I told him that I would make a deal with you. He set back in his chair and said I'm listen. If you get her to sign up and they approve her. I will pay first and last month rent at any two bed room apartment of your chose. I could see he was thinking about it. Then he said some where nice. I jumped right in and said you got to pay your rent every month. He looked at me and said bet. Then I asked Jap if he wanted to get down with the team? Jap said dame right boss it's about money. Then I heard slow called me back in the kitchen. When I got back there the pickle jar was on full. Slow was smiling from ear to ear then he was putting gray tape around the jar. Then he took a hammer and started breaking the glass around the dope. When he pulled the tape off the jar. There was no glass on the dope. That move there fucked me up all the glass was on the tape. After we got everything together slow called his uncle from the basement and gave him a peace to try.

After he smoked it he told us that it was good and it had a great after taste. I asked him what did it taste like? He said that it was sweet. gave Slow a zip and a half. I gave Jap a zip. Then I gave Everyday two zips. Then I told them that I needed eighteen a zip. I told slow that half he had was all him for the work he done on that stove. That left me with three and a half zips for myself. I called white boy and ten minutes later he was there. I told Everyday not to forget what I told him earlier that night about the project move. When I got in the car I asked White boy if he fucked with that white girl. He said yeah then I reached up front and gave him a nice peace. When I made it home I wasn't in the house for ten minutes when I heard the door bell ring. When I looked out of the window it was White boy. He told me that he had a hundred dollars for some more of that. I gave him five for eighty and told him to keep twenty for his self.

I went to school for a week and didn't see Every day, Jap or Slow. That next Monday I was walking down the hallway and herd Jap call me. When I saw him I said dame man I thought you quit school. He said Rose I been getting that money playa. I asked him if he seen Slow or Every day? He said yeah they are here. I told him to meet me at lunch time and to tell the guys. He said ok then I went to class. After two classes later I went to the lunch room and they all were there at the table. When I walked up I was glad to see my guys. What's up play boys? When I set down I told them to clear the table it's about business right now. People at the table were tripping, because I was a lower classman. Every day, Slow and Jap cleared it up real quick.

When I sat down it was only four of us at the table now. I asked them what was popping? They all started paying me my money. Slow gave me eighteen hundred. Jap gave me eighteen hundred and Every day gave me thirty six hundred. All together I picked up seventy two hundred I had a nice Monday. When they was moving that money across the table that white girl the new teacher was watching everything from across the room. I asked Every day about that business with his girl? He told me that it was done she is on the waiting list now. Then I told them to get beepers and car phones after school today. Then we all made our move out of the lunch room. I made it half way down the hall when she stopped me and said you told me that you where new here. I said I was to you. Then she said my name DANYON. I asked her how did you know my name? She smiled and said the first day we met on the steps and you jumped into that pretty B.M.W. I had to know your name. So I asked a couple of teachers about you. Once I told them about how you dress they knew who I was talking about. I asked her was the teachers males are females? She smiled again and said females. Then she asked me why did I ask? I told her that the men here give me a hard time. They say that I think I'm too cool around here. Then she asked me how old I was? I told her that age was nothing, but a number. Then I told her that I was sixteen. She looked me up and down and said that I was a big sixteen years old.

I said all over and she said yeah right. At this time the hallway was clear we were the only two people in it. Then she asked me who was the woman, that picks me up? I told her that Honey was my woman. Then she asked how old was she? I said twenty three. She said that she is older then me. Then I asked her how was she? She looked at me and said that was none of my business. Then she asked me what did my forks have to say about all this? I looked at her and baby girl I'm grown. I have my own house and my own life. I do what I want when I want.

When I got tired of all these games I turned around and walked away. When I got down the hall I heard her say that is a lot of money to make in five minutes at a lunch table. I turned the corner and went into the gym. I knew that was the class Every day had. I asked him if I could use his car to drop this money off. He gave me his keys and told me where he parked at. I walked right out the side door. When I found his car Jap Slow and Every day parked right beside each other. Something told me to turn around and look up. When I did I saw the new teacher on the fourth floor looking out of the window looking down at me. She shook her head at me. I smiled and wave at her and jumped in the I—rock and turned the music up and pulled off.

I made it home right on time because Honey was about to pull out to come get me. I blocked her in the driveway and told her to come in for a minute. I told her what went down in the hallway at school. I gave her the money. I went in the well and grab three more oz's or zips as we call them. I gave the three zips to Honey and told her to drive the I—rock behind me to school. I jumped into the B.M.W and honey drove the I—rock and we headed back to school. When we pulled up Every day was just walking out of school. He saw Honey in his car and me in mind. As he walked up to me I kept the window up. Honey blew the horn and he walked to his car. She got out and told him that there was three zips in a bag under the seat. There is one for each of you. He told her ok and got into his car. When Honey was coming to get in the car with me I saw the new teacher on the steps just watching her. I didn't know what to think, she didn't say if would tell on me.

As I thought about it she was asking me question like she was trying to get with me. I know what I need to do today. I picked up the phone and called Velt. When he picked up I asked him for Eye's number? He asked me what was going on? I told him that I have to talk to him later on in the game right now is not the time. He said ok then gave me the number. I called Eye's up and told him that I needed some information on someone. He asked me the name. I told him that I didn't have it. He asked me if I had a address. I told him that I didn't. Then he asked me if I had a plate number. I told him to let me call him right back and he said ok. I made a u turn and went back to school. I parked and waited about a block away. She came out around three o'clock. When she pulled out of the parking lot I pulled up right behind her and Honey wrote down her plate number. Then I made a right turn and called Eye's back and gave him the info he needed.

She was driving a B.M.W to the same kind we had. Eye's called back and said that he would give me the info I wanted when I drop off his money. He charged me four hundred for the info. I told him that I would come through later on tonight then I huge the phone up.

As I was driving we rolled by a car lot and I saw it. It was a nineteen eighty seven El co. it was mid night blue like the B.M.W. I pulled over and went into the building and asked them how much did they wanted for it? He looked at me and said twelve thousand. I told him that I could give him eighty five hundred for it right now. The sale man said to day. I told him to start the paper work. I'll be back in twenty minutes. He said bet. I told Honey to stay and do the paper work in her name. I ran home and got some more money. When I pulled back up Honey was done with the paper work.

The sale man handed me the keys. I went straight to the D.M.V and got my plates. I left there and went to the rime shop and bought some chrome Dayton rims. Then I went to get a phone put in it. The car had a paint job on it. Tomorrow all I had to do is get some tint and some sounds. When I pulled back up to the house Honey, said that the car was beautiful. I really loved the power it had. I know why the car runs like a scarred dog and it had the pipes running out the back of it. When I pulled up to the school the next day it was like that. I pulled onto the parking lot. They were parked on the side of the lot.

Every day Jap and Slow was on my nuts like clockwork. She was in the window looking down at me once again. When I saw her it made me think about Eye's. Dam I forgot to drop in on him last night to get that info. Every day walked up to the car and got in. He told me that his girl got approve for the apartment. I told him that was quick. He said that her people work down there. Then I asked him when did he want to go apartment hunting? He told me when I was ready. I asked him to give me a couple of days. He said ok play boy. The bell rang and we went on in to school. After my second class I saw her in the hallway. She walked up on me and said that it look like I didn't want to see her or something. I told her look lady I don't have time for all this bullshit today. I don't even know your name. She started to say something I walked away to my next class. When I turned the corner I saw her standing there looking at me with her arms cross. When lunch time came I was walking and saw her coming towards me I made a left and walked out of the fort door and jumped in my car.

I had to see Eye's today anyway no better time, then right now. I walked into Eye's office. He was an old fat white man with thick ass glasses. The glasses made his eyes big that's why we call him eyes. The first thing he said to me was, where the fuck was you last night? I know your father. I know he raised you better than that. I told Eye's I was so sorry and it will not happen again. Then he asked me if I had that money for him. I said yeah man you know it. As I gave it to him he passed me a folder. Her name was Kim Peters. Age twenty two years of age single no kids, went to college in main. She lives out there by Velt and I have her phone number. I told him thanks. I jumped back in the ride and went back to school lunch was almost over. When I walked back into school she was standing by the side door. She didn't see me slide in. When she looked up I was at the table with Every day and the crew. She walked up and told me to come here and I walked away with her. I said Kim every time I turn around I see you. Do you like what you see? Before she could say something I asked another question. I said Kim know what I like what I see. You need to let me show you around

Detroit. Then she asked me how did I know that she wasn't from here? You are from back east, main right? You are single and the only child. Your father name is Jim and your mother name is Sally. Your father is a doctor and your mom is a third grade teacher. You are twenty two then the bell rang and I walked off. She had a blink look on her face all day she just looked at me. I guess she was trying to put two and two together. After school we were in the parking lot when I heard my phone ringing. I picked it up and hello. It was Honey she asked me where was I at? I said school why? She said that something bad had happen.

I said what, she told me that Pat has been shot and big sunny was killed out there in Nebraska. I asked her when did this happen? She said this morning. Then I asked her where was she at? She told me that she was at Velt's house. Then I asked her how was Velt taking it? She said I haven't seen him like this since your father was killed. I asked her did anyone tell Tarzan? She said him and his crew on their way out there right now. I told her that I was on my way right now as soon as I hung the phone up and lifted my head up and saw lil sunny boy. I told him to come here. He told me to hold up I told Jap and Slow to go grab that nigga by his neck and bring him to me right now. Right fucking now!!

At the same time I jumped in the ride and pulled out of the parking spot. Jap and slow had him like a rag doll by his neck and brought him to me. They threw him in the ride and I mashed the fuck out. He was mad and asked me what the fuck was going on? Your daddy and Pat got shot up this morning. He asked me when did I find out? I told him just now on the parking lot. Honey called me on my car phone. Then he asked me if he could use the phone I said yeah. Then he called home and when his mom picked up I could hear him ask her why was she crying? She must have said that he was gone. Because he asked her who was gone? That's when she dropped the hole world on my guy shoulder. She said that Big sunny was shot in the head this morning. He asked her how bad was it? And she said that he was dead baby. I saw sunny head drop down.

Then he lifted his hands up to his face and started to yell why. I can't say anything I have been there. He asked me where were we going? I told him that we were going over Velt house too caught up with Tarzan them. We were about ten minutes out. It was quite in the car. Sunny wasn't saying anything, I can say that I saw sunny turn in to a man right in front of me. His sadness turned into anger, then, he said Rosewood I got to handle this for my old dude playa. I still didn't say anything, I turned into the driveway. We made it past the trees there were cars everywhere and two niggas standing outside the front door. I called in the house and told them I was outside on my phone, cause I never seen these two niggas before. When Tarzan opened the door, we got out the car and walked in. There were people all over the house Sunny boy's people were there too. He saw his uncle Nutty in the living room with his crew. These cats were like Tarzan and his crew, they were the pressers in the game. I was looking for Velt, when I found him he was on the phone getting info from playas in Nebraska.

When he got off the phone, he called the hitters to the front room and started telling everyone what was going on and what happened before all this went down. He said, the word on the street was that Pat and Sunny took over the niggas set. Then the nigga girlfriend chose up on Pat. When he was getting that dope from Tarzan he was the man to fuck with. He had the lowest prices in the game up there. The niggas tried to fight them over the weekend in the club. Sunny popped three niggas in the club that night. They laid low for the next two days, some way they got both of them together at a bar-b-que spot this morning.

They were still in their cars when they pined them in, then niggas opened fire at them. They say Sunny got hit twenty times, Pat crawled under the dash board of his car. Nutty asked Velt what was the niggas name that run it? Velt said, Coco, Nutty said he's my bitch. Then Sunny boy said, no he's my bitch. Nutty said, Sunny boy I'm going to make you stand on that.

Sunny fucked me up and said, like a rock play boy. Then he told all the people that wasn't getting their hands dirty must leave the room at this time. Velt look at me and I told Honey to leave the room. Candy and Jet stood by Velt's side.

CHAPTER TEN

When I Made My Bones

When we left velt said, we were pulling out in and hour. Everyone should meet back up at big mama's house. Sunny boy caught a ride back with his uncle nutty. I trailed honey home, when we got there she asked me why did I put her out of the room? I told her that I had some business to handle here. Then I said baby I know that you are a gangsta! But I need you to find us some where to stay, because when we come back you know that pat and his woman is coming back too. She said shit, I forgot about that baby. I called every day and told him to get that money from everyone and give it to hi girl to give to honey. I wanted him to let honey talk to her so they could go apartment hunting starting tomorrow. He said okay, then he asked me what was up? I said that I had to go out of town for a few days, I passed the phone to honey, then started getting my things together for the trip. Honey came in the room and said, that she and everyday baby's mama will start looking tomorrow. I told her that everyday would have fifty four hundred for me in a couple of days. She said okay baby, I will get that for you. Please be careful out there baby, I said I will baby. I will get home as soon as I can. Honey walked upon me and hugged me.

Then I heard the door bell rang, when I opened it was Nutty and Sunny Boy, as I was talking to them Tarzan and Roosevelt hit the corner. I turned to honey and told her that I loved her. I walked out to the car, Tarzan, Roosevelt, Nutty and Sunny Boy were standing in a group talking. Velt asked me if I was riding with him Candy and Jet? I said No because I was driving my own car. Then I remembered something, and ran back into the house told honey to get my phone book and an about three thousand. She asked me why did I need my phone book? I told her that I could drop in on pimp Sue in Iowa and handle some business. I can kill two birds with one stone. I then went to my spot and grabbed a half of a brick. When I made it outside everyone had made it. I told Sunny Boy to come and ride with me.

When we pulled out I was between Roosevelt and Tarzan at the front of the pack. When we were on the highway in the middle of the night, I couldn't do nothing but think but think about my old dude. This is how they came to St. Louis, that night. I bet I was like Pat spot in the line of cars, Sunny Boy was quite I know the feeling, I can say to him I know how you feel, and really know how he felt We pulled into Nebraska around nine o'clock Roosevelt, Tarzan, Nutty, Candy, Jet and Sunny Boy went to the hospital to see Pat. I went to the car rental store to with Roosevelt's card to get a car. The guy on the spot was one of Roosevelt's customers. I went back to the motel to get some rest.

About an hour went past when everyone came back, I was sleep by then, I was rolling over when Sunny Boy walked in, he told me that Pat would be alright. I said that's cool then I asked him what happen? He told me what had went down. That was some cold shit too, Sunny Boy looked at me and said that's okay we gonna deal with it the same way they did. I just sat there and looked at him. Sunny Boy didn't look right in the eyes any more. He looked cold now, around two o'clock we all got up everyone but me and Sunny Boy went to see Pat again. Sunny Boy and I hit the streets in the rental. We had a name Coco, we was all over the city, car washes, parks, ma and pa stores. We didn't say much when we started Sunny wanted to ask everyone did they know Coco? I told him that was not the way just lay on back and keep your eyes open.

We were at our sixth car wash when I overheard a nigga talking about meeting Coco at the club tonight. I walked up on the nigga and asked him what kinda paint did he have on his SS? He told me and we talked about cars for a minute. I pulled out a honey blunt and fired it up. The nigga asked what was I smoking? I told him a honey blunt, he said that's all weed, I said yeah. I asked him did he want to hit it? He said yeah he hit it a few times. Then he asked us where were we from? Sunny Boy said, we are from De—Before he could finish I said Denver, Denver, mile high baby. He said that we had some fire weed. I asked him were did they party around there. He said shit my boy Coco throwing a party tonight. Why don't you come. I said Coco she want mind would she?

He started to laugh and said Coco is the man around town, I said the man, he said yeah, the man. I said do you think that he would like to buy some works from Denver? He said dam right, we need another connect. I asked what happen to your last connect? If you don't mind me asking, He said they got their asses killed, I said playboy I am from Denver, and we didn't play that. He said chill out home boy these cat were from Detroit. Sunny Boy said Detroit! Then I said them Detroit niggas are something else. Play Boy we have been here for about an hour, my name is June, and this is my brother S.B.

He said my name is Yellow, the club name is The Spot, come around one o'clock tonight, I said bet. Then he tried to hand me back the blunt, I told him he could have it. He said that cool. Man you cool ass people, I said, you to man. I will see you tonight, play boy. He said alright home boy. Then he pulled off the lot. When we made it back to the motel everyone was back. Trazan an Nutty walked up to us and said, yall go out joy riding, but you can't go and see Pat. I said is he alright? Tarzan said yeah. I said shit I didn't have to see him then. I'm on something else, then I asked Trazan and Nutty did they have some more info on what happen? They said that he told us the same thing as yesterday. I told them that I was meeting Coco tonight at a club called the spot. He thinks that I'm from Denver, I'm a D boy with some works to let go. Nutty asked me how I did it? Then Sunny Boy started telling everyone how I pulled it off. I went back to bed.

A hour later candy came in my room and told me that Velt wanted to see me. I got up in my boxers and ask Candy to pass me my pants. She looked down and said boy you got the right name (wood) I looked down and saw that my shit was hanging out and it was hard. Then she said I know what Honey walks bow legget now. Shit I might fall in love with that too. I told her to get her nasty ass out of my room. She stepped toward me and grabbed a hand full of my shit. Then she kissed me on my check. She went down on me slow, when I looked down she was looking at me. She still had my shit in her hand, then she put it in her mouth, it was hot and wet, I closed my eyes for a second and saw Honey's face. When I open them I was looking at Honey,

I saw Candy getting down like she live. I pushed her down on the floor and went to the bath room. To finish getting my thing off, at that moment in time I knew that I really loved Honey. When I came out of the bath, Candy was gone when I made it to Velt's room she was sitting on the couch with her legs crossed. When I set down on the bed across from her, she smiled and uncrossed her legs. She didn't have on any under wear, her cat was fat then she reached between her legs and stuck her finger in her cat. When she pulled it out she stuck her finger in her drink. Then she crossed her legs again, then she put her finger in her mouth. I told her she was a nasty bitch Velt said Rose you just tripping off that? She's a freak but what we have isn't about love. I love what she do for me but I don't love that ho. I'm surprise you Ain't hit that ass yet. Candy said I tried to give him some pussy but that nigga in love with Honey. Velt said that's a good thing if it true. But he is still young right now. I want to see him in about twenty years from now. I said man, you woke me up for this bullshit? Velt said chill out playa, how are you going to handle that business tonight? I said that I wanted to take Tarzan, Nutty, and Sunny Boy with me tonight. He said that's cool, but I'm going to send Candy and Jet with them guns in the club before you all go in. They gonna be on yell like white on rice playa. So when yell walk in play it cool and find Coco. You know they are worried about how we are coming. I said that when I talked to that nigga yellow he was like that wasn't nothing. Velt said you got to understand Coco is the king on this board. Yellow could just be a pawn on board.

Do you want to hit them there? I said that would be the best spot. Then Tarzan walked in and asked what was going on? Velt brought him up to speed, then asked me why would that be the best spot? I said that there would be so many people there doing their own thing. When we do him everyone will take off for the doors, then we can slide right out with the crowd. Tarzan, then asked me was I up for this? I said that when that happen to my old dude he did it for me. I'm there for him now. Velt said that he was going to get a cab for Candy and Jet. We could follow the cab from the motel to the club.

Tarzan then left to go tell Nutty and Sunny Boy the play. Velt asked me if I wanted to play a game of chess. I said okay we played about three games. We had about a half hour left. The girls was ready the cab was on the way. It came and the mission was a go. The club was popping the parking lot was full. We watched candy and Jet walk right in. They had a body dresses on they were showing everything. The guards, at the door was tripping of their ass and they didn't even search them. But when we hit the door they were all over our asses. Asking us where we was from and things like that. Nutty started to say that he was from De—I jumped in again and said that we were from Denver. We were invited by Yellow, one guard said speak of the devil. Yellow hit the corner and said June what's up home boy? I said shit don't look like we aint going to get in play boy. He said come on and we walked straight in. The club was dark and smokey, there were people everywhere. Along the wall there was a row of booths we followed Yellow through the crowd and made our way to the VIP section. We had to step up three steps to be on the same level with everyone else. When I looked around I saw Candy and Jet setting in VIP section with two nigga s already. I said to myself these ho's here are something else. I'm glad that they are on my team. Yellow walked up to Coco and said What's up home boy. These are the two cats I told you about earlier today. Coco said what up niggas?

I started to say my name when he cut me off and told two more niggas to search us again. I said dam man I should have came here butt naked! Candy and Jet started laughing. Coco told them to shut the fuck up. I said baby girls you would do better fucking with some plays from Denver. We know how to treat women at our spot. We know when we aren't wanted either, This is bad business fuck this!! I'm the nigga with the work you got me feeling like you got the work. His cat was done, then he said they clean, He stood up and started to talk, I turned my back to him and walked off. I heard Candy tell Jet that's a real nigga there. Candy then said, hold up baby can I get a dance from you. I turned around and said come on with your sexy self. We walked to the dance floor with my arm around her waist. We started dancing I kept my back toward them she was watching their moves and telling me what she saw in my car. I grab two nines from between her thighs. They were holding seventeen rounds a piece, Jet had the same thing on her too, Tarzan was dancing with her too. Candy told me that Yellow was talking to Coco, I asked her could she pick up on what they were saying. She said no because the music was too loud. But they are keeping their eyes on you, I would bet the house on it. Shit he is coming this way, I said who? She said Coco, I said that if they call us back to the booth you and Jet say that you got to go to the bathroom. Then go get the ride the keys are in the glove box. She said ok, than I felt a tap on my shoulder. When I turned around it was Coco. I said dam man you want us to leave too? He said come on back to the booth so we can talk about some business. When I started to walk away from the dance floor, candy told Jet lets go to the bathroom girl. I told Coco, man you got some fine bitches around here. He said yeah we do. When I walked pass Tarzan, I gave him that look Sunny Boy walked up on the other side of me. I slid them one of the guns that I had. I saw another girl walk past me I grab her hand and stop to talk to her. Coco turned to see what I was doing, at the same time Sunny Boy, Tarzan and

Nutty kept walking to the booth. Coco told me to come on, I said okay playa. I started back walking towards the booth. I told Coco I heard good things about him. We were about five feet from the booth.

When I saw Sonny Boy walking toward us, I grabbed another girl hand and spend off with her. Coco turned his head to see what I was doing. Then I heard Sunny Boy call out his name Coco!! WHEN Coco turned his head back toward Sunny Boy, Then Sunny Boy shot four times Bang! Bang! Bang! Bang! I saw blood jump out of Coco chest like in the movies. Tarzan and Nutty started popping niggas in the booth. All I heard was Bang, Bang, Bang, Bang, Bang, Bang, Bang, Bang, Bang, Bang, Bang, Bang, Bang, Bang!!!

I turned my eyes back to Coco laying on the floor. I walked up on him and bent down over him and said this is from Pat! I called Sunny Boy over, when he heard the name Sunny Boy his eyes got big. I stood back up and put my gun in his face, Sunny Boy put his gun in his face too. I closed my eyes and pulled the trigger, sunny Boy and I didn't stop pulling the trigger till it quit. Nutty and Tarzan grabbed up and rushed us out of the door with the rest of the crowd. Candy and Jet was waiting for us outside, we made it back to the motel we all threw our clothes away. Me and Sunny Boy got cleaned up, ten minutes after everything went down Sunny Boy and I were on the highway to Iowa to see pimp Sue. Roosevelt told me later that the police came to the hospital to question Pat but he was cool because he was on the books for being there. A hour later he checked out. Velt, took him and his girl friend back to Detroit.

Five hours later we were pulling into Iowa City. I called pimp Sue on the way up here. I pulled in a lot of apartments, I saw pimp Sue lack. I blew the horn a few times, Then, I saw the lights flash on and off a couple of times. Then I saw Sue, I parked and we walked in the apartment, we talked for a minute then I said let's get down to business. I asked him did he get what I told him to get. He said yeah. Then he told me to follow him to the kitchen, he had everything set up. I had to show him how to work the magic on the stove. I turned eight into sixteen I get him eight and charge him forty six thousand a zip. But in Iowa they were slanging a rock for fifty dollars all day long. Shit he didn't have no problem with it because he didn't buy anything I gave it to him.

He was making money hand over fist; I told him that I would be sending someone to get my money in a month and a half. He said okay I will have that thirty seven thousand for you Rosewood. I told him it's all good pimp Sue, the next day I headed back to Detroit. The last couple days Sunny Boy didn't say anything. That wasn't like him, we were on the highway when he said Rosewood, I said what's up pimping? He said that he wanted in my little family. I looked at him then I asked him what did he want to do? His answer fucked me up, he told me that he wanted to be my head knocker. I said what? Sunny, he said that night at the club I enjoyed myself playa. Let me have your back. I only fuck with you!

I told him to give me some time to think about it. He said it's like this play, if I don't work for you I will work for someone in the game. I have found my trade in the game, so think about it play boy. Shit I couldn't say nothing but just think about what he is asking me for, shit in the club sunny Boy wasn't bull shiting he kept it gangsta. We were about an hour outside of Detroit, when I called Honey. A woman answer the phone she said hello, I said Honey there she said Honey doesn't live here. Then she hung the phone up. I called back and she answered the phone again, I asked her who the fuck was she? She asked me who the fuck was I? I told her that bitch this is Rosewood. She said I don't know no mother. Then she was cut off. I heard Pat on the phone say lil Rose, I said Pat, he said yeah. I ask him who was that bitch.

He said Man that's my girl. I said she's a trip play boy. He said that's why I told you what I told you the last time I was here. I asked him where is Honey? He said that she left a number to the new apartment. He gave it to me, and I called it she wasn't there. Then I called the car phone she picked it up, I said what's up baby girl? She said nigga I been worried about yo ass. Everyone has been back for a couple of days now. I said that I told you that I was going to see pimp Sue before I came home. She said I know baby you could have called me or something, I said baby, I had a lot of shit on my mine. I needed that time to think. She said I can understand where you are coming from, How far are you? I said about a hour out. She gave me the address to the new apartment. I asked her about the business with Everyday, She said that they moved and that they are waiting on you to give them some more. I asked her did she get that shit out of the wall. She said yeah, I said why didn't you give it to them? She said you didn't tell me too. I said you are right baby. Did you find them an apartment? She said yeah, they are on the third floor and we are on the ninth floor.

I told her that I would be home after I drop Sunny of at home. She said baby I can't wait to see you. I said Honey you don't know how much, I missed you! I hung up the phone Sunny Boy asked me what's up play boy? I said Sunny Boy, that's a hard job, what if I have a problem with one of your friends and I tell you to smoke him? What would you do? He said I would smoke his ass. Because I know that a nigga would have to be in the wrong, when you tell me to go to work. I looked at him and said Sunny are you sure? He said as a heart attack, I told him that he had the job. When I pulled up in front of his house I gave him a thousand dollars. I told him that I would come and get him Monday morning for school. He said bet. Then he gave the money back to me and said Rosewood I need a car playa. I looked at him and said Sunny that move there is what legends are made of. He smiled and said yeah, I'm a legend that's walking everywhere all over the city. I said shit they had to start somewhere. When I pulled up in front of the building I saw that it was nice. We had off street parking under the building that was cool too. When I made it to our floor I tripped at how nice it was, I felt like one of the Jefferson shit we were moving up in the game. I liked Honey taste, this was her first apartment as well. I knocked on the door, then I saw the door bell I pushed it. Then I heard my baby's sweet voice on the other side of the door. Then I knew that I was home, It wasn't about the address if Honey was there then it was home to me.

She opened the door and jumped right into my arms. She was kissing me just like I had just got back from world war two or something. I can't lie it felt so good to be in her arms. Honey made me feel so loved and wanted. Between me and you, she made me feel safe in her arms. When I walked in I looked around at our place, I was set up real nice, when you walked in you were in the living room, the kitchen was to the left, they had a breakfast bar in it with all of the appliances in it. At the back wall of the living room was a big bay window and glass sliding door. I looked out of the window we had a nice view. The bathroom was kind of small but we could work with it. I went to the right of the living room this was the bedroom. She had a king size bed in it, the room was all bed, and she had the people at the store bring a big screen television placed at the end of the bed. I was right, I looked at Honey, I could see that she was looking for my approval. I said the bathroom is too small, and the closet is too. I don't know but I know one thing. She said what's that? I said, I like it!! She started jumping up and down saying for real you do. I said Yeah, I love it I'm proud of you.

Chapter Eleven

Perfecting My Hustle

Today I got up early and got dress, honey was still in the bed. I leaned over and gave her a kiss on her cheek. I called Sunny Boy to tell him that I was on my way. When I got outside I remembered Everyday's apartment number. I buzz it a couple of times his girl answer the call she said hello, I said is everyday up? She said who is this? I said Rosewood, She said how are you doing? Then asked me when are we going to meet? I said later on baby girl ok. She said ok. Then I heard Every day in the background. He asked her who was that? I told him that it was me. He said Rosewood, I said yeah man, He asked me when did I get in? I told him last night. I told him to call up the boys and tell them to meet me at the school in the lunch room as soon as they can. He said alright, than he said I can ride with you. I told him that I had something before school I'll just met you there. He told me that he was on it.

Then I jumped in my car to go get Sunny boy. When I pulled up Sunny was standing on the front ready to go. When he got in the car I asked him how was his mom doing? He said okay he guess. Then went on to say that she wasn't talking to any one for real I looked at him and said that I could understand that. He shook his head and said me too. Then I asked him what was up with you? He told me that he couldn't sleep last night, because he kept seeing coco's face.

Then he asked me if I had some weed? I said yeah and we smoked one on the way to school. When we made it to school we were both high as a kite. When we walked in the lunch room I went to the table and sunny went to the lunch line to get something to eat. When I made it to the table Everyday was smiling from ear to ear. I asked him what the fuck was he smiling for? He said man you are a real ass nigga. I said yeah you just tripping off it now. He said no man I love my apartment. I looked that him and said you talking like I was on some bullshit or something? At first I thought you were. Then I asked him was he cool? He told me shit I'm cool. Then Sunny boy walked up and set down. Jap and slow told him he had to go. I told them that sunny boy was inn. They stopped and looked at me. Then I asked them if they had a problem? They all said no, then I went on to tell them that he was family now. So respect him as such.

Everyday was the first to give him love. Then Jap and Slow fell right in line. Then I asked them to keep there eyes open for another I—Rock. Jap asked for you? I said no for Sunny boy. Slow said that he knew where one was right now. I asked him how much was it? He said eighty five hundred. I told Sunny that he had to fix it up by yourself and I want my money back A.S.A.P. He looked at me and said ok. Then I told everyone after school we would check it out. Sunny boy was smiling like it was his birthday. Then the ball rang and we all went to class. It was five minutes to two. I grab the hall pass to go to the rest room. As I was coming out of the rest room I ran into her. She asked me how was I doing? I said fine. Then I asked her how are you doing Kim? She said I'm ok, but I can be better. I asked her in what way? Tell me and let me see if I can help you with your problem. She started smiling and said, I wasn't suppose to say that out loud. I told her that it will stay between us. I can hold water, the question is can you? Then the bell rang and I took off. I had some business to take care of. Sunny saw us talking and asked me what was the teacher was talking about? I told him that it didn't cost a dime to stay out of mine. He started laughing and said ok Rosewood. We all went to the lot to check out the car for Sunny boy. It was cool I told the sale man to get it ready we will pick it up tomorrow. Then I told Jap to take Sunny home. I told Everyday to follow me to the house. I had some business to talk over him at his apartment.

When I walked in Everyday apartment it was laid out. I found out later that Honey had took his girl friend shopping for the stuff in there home. As I set down on the couch in his front room he went in to the kitchen. He asked me what was up? I told him about the move I made with Sunny boy. He said, man I trust you, you know your hand that you are trying to play. So you tell me, what is Sunny boys job? I said that he is my head knocker, Everyday looked at me with mouth wide open. He stopped in his tracks and said do you know if he would get down, I said yeah play boy. It fucked me up when I seen it myself, now what's really fucked up about it is that he liked it. You should have seen his eye's, every time he pulled the trigger his eyes lit up like the fourth of July.

But he knows that I would get down to. Everyday said, what did you go do? I said, don't worry about it play boy. What's up with the apartment in the projects? He said, that it was cool it's on the tenth floor. Is that the top floor? I asked. He said yeah a corner spot. I asked him what was up with the players down there? He said that he knows a couple of nigga that live down there. So what are you telling me I said Everyday said that he would go check the vibe out tomorrow. I said what's up with tonight, he said alright tonight I told him to call me on the car phone later.

The next day came after school I gave Sunny boy the money to go get his car today. I told Every day, Jap, and Slow to go with him. I also told them to show him how to get plates on his car. Later on I tripped off of it, I was showing him things that his father was going to show him. I was on my way home when Honey called me on the car phone. I said what's up? She said that Pat had called and wants you to call him. I said ok then hung the phone up. I called Pat and his girl answered the phone. She said, hello I asked is Pat there? She said who is this? Rosewood I answered, she said what do you want? I just hung up the phone. A week later Velt called me and told me that they were going to have a party for Pat at big mama's house. He asked me was I coming I said, yeah. Honey asked me are we going to Pat's party? I said, I'm cool I'm not going, but you can go if you want to. She said, no I'm staying with you. The next night Velt called me and said, are you on your way?

I said, no I'm cool I'm going to watch T.V with Honey and chill in the crib. I heard Velt tell Pat that he wasn't coming over. Pat said, he won't return my phone calls or nothing. What's up with him? Velt said, Rosewood Pat wanted to know what's going on. I told him that I'm busy I'll holla later on in the game. Then I hung the phone up. I told Honey to get dressed, she asked me are we going over to Pat's house? I said, no we're going out to dinner and to the movies. I called Every day, Jap, Slow, and Sunny boy and told them to meet me at the movies and to bring their girls so we can kick it. Sunny boy has stepped up over the last week, he even had a girl. I must say we kicked it.

Two weeks later Velt called me up and said that he was putting together a party this weekend and wanted me to come. I asked him who all was coming over? He said, Pat and his woman, Tarzan and a few other playas, I told him thanks but no thanks I'm going out of town this weekend. He asked where I was going, I told him Iowa to see pimp Sue. I got some business to handle up that way. He said, when you gonna come see me? I told him when I get back then I hung the phone up. I picked it back up and called Sunny boy, I told him to pack some clothes it's time to go see pimp Sue. He said cool when? Tonight playa, I said.

I hung him up, then called Honey and told her to get the last out. She said I thought you forgot about that. I said I didn't I was holding that for pimp Sue. I'm going that way tonight, so pack you some clothes. She said, I'm going too I said yeah. I need you to get the rental car too. I will be home about a half hour she said ok. Then I called Everyday and told him to call Hen-C and tell him that I wanted to get a brick in about two days. Then I told him to get the apartment ready in the jets. Tell Jap and Slow to watch the nigga down there and see how they move.

When I get back its time to set up shop. He said, what about Sunny boy? I said he is with on this run, he said okay I got you all around the board playa. I pulled up in front of the crib, Honey came down the stairs. I parked the Elco and got in the B.M.W Honey was looking good today. Don't get me wrong she is always looking good. I told her that we leave tonight, I need you to drive the rental up to Iowa. You cool with that, she said yeah daddy. They are with me right, I said yeah baby. She said, I need to get something little and pretty a girls car. I dropped her off at the rental place. I told her to go back to the apartment and put the shit in the rental. She said ok kissed me then I pulled off.

I was on my way to get Sunny boy, when I pulled up on him he was on the front sitting on the hood of his car. When I pulled up the girls he was talking to just looked at me. I pulled right right up behind his car, music bumping. I called him on his car phone, he picked it up I told him to go get his shit and lets ride homeboy. He said nigga you a fool, I told him I like sitting behind this blue tint. He came out and threw his shit in the car. When he opened the door the girls was trying to look off in the car to see who was pushing it. I pulled off and headed to the projects to take a look around. When I hit the lot I saw Jap, and Slow in Jap's ride, I rode past them slowly, Sunny boy asked me why I didn't stop? I told him that we were all down here on business. I called Jap and told him what to look for, the main thing I want to know is who the top dog is. Jap told me that he feel me on that, I came back by them on the way out and jumped back on the high way to go home.

When I made it home Every day was out front helping Honey load the rental car. That was right on time. When I got out the car I walked up to Everyday and asked him what did Hen-C say. He said that he was going to hold one for you, he's at the end of it but he got you. He also said holla at him when you get some time, that was it playa. I told Everyday that I just came from the projects, he said I told Jap and Slow to get there ass up and go do that. I told him to calm down they were down there on the job, I just wanted to tell you good job play boy. He said thanks Rosewood then I told Sunny boy to go chill with Everyday for a few hours. We moving at eight o'clock. Sunny boy asked me what was I going to do? I said I'm going to sleep me and Honey.

Honey woke me up around seven thirty that night, I got up and took a bath, Honey had already cooked. I put my clothes on when I walked outside Everyday and Sunny boy were already there. I pulled out and Honey was behind me in the rental. It took us about ten hours to get there. When we pulled up in pimp Sue was ready the money count was right and I had another package for him. We spent the night the next day Sunny boy drove back the rental with the money in it. Honey rode with me, Sunny boy was right behind me. We made it back to Detroit late that evening I have to say that was a good trip. When I made it back in the house I called Hen-C and told him tomorrow it was about us. He said cool, then I told Sunny boy to take the rental car home I'll get it from him tomorrow. He said ok and left after we unloaded it. We finally made it in the apartment I called Every day I asked him what was up? He told me to come over and talk with him. I told him I was coming down right now, he said alright then hung up.

When I got there he was already at the door I heard a females voice say that's him. It was Everyday's baby momma she was bad too. This was my second time seeing her, the first time I didn't trip off of her because I had a lot on my mind. When I walked in he said, how was the trip boss? I said that it was good. Then I told him that we had business to handle with C tomorrow. He said that's good, and that his money was getting funny. I looked over his shoulder and his girl friend was looking at me. So I asked Everyday if they had something for a head ache. She said hold on then she came back with something. I said, thank you she smiled I asked Everyday would that hold him till we get everything on track. He said yeah I'm cool playa, I said good when we get back on I'm going to need that back. He looked and said okay. Then he said, Rose we are ready to go the spot is ready. The door is still open with the road behind it. We have a peep hole. The room is just like you said, Jap and Slow has pushed up on a couple of girls. They are ready to move in on the sixth and third floors of the building. I said that's cool we can pull shifts now. He said that for a couple of hundred a week, we can get a look out all over the projects. I said, tomorrow we will go buy some walkie talkies and a police scanner. He looked at me and said that's right on time. I said where is the baby boy at? He said that he is over his mother s house. His girlfriend said, it's so quite around here. I said better yet you can get the stuff today. Take a couple hundred out and give it to me.

When he gave it to me. I asked him would he mind if I gave that to your woman. He said no I called her over and asked her what was her name? she said Pam. I said Pam this is for you to take your man out today ok. She said I don't know. I said, you and him are going out to spend the day together anyway. Everyday said, we are? I said, yeah you are. You have to go get my stuff don't you. Take her with you and go do something with her nigga. He laughed and said alright dad.

I got up and went up stairs. When I walked in the door Honey was on the phone. She said here he go, then she gave me the phone. I said hello, it was Pat he asked me what's up? I said man what do you want? He said, damn what's up with that. I hung the phone up and told Honey when he calls back tell him I'm sleep. Two seconds later the phone rang. Pat said, put Rose on the phone Honey told him I was in the bed. He told her to put me on the phone. She said, my man is in the bed call back then she hung up the phone. After school the next day it was on Every day, Sunny boy, and myself went to see Hen-C. Jap and Slow moved in the Pj's. I was driving the B.M.W to day, I had to show Hen-C that I was getting paper. When we pulled up at his car wash Everyday was in front of me, Sunny boy was in the back. They were both in the I—Roc's Honey was already on the parking lot getting the rental washed. Every day and Sunny boy got out and walked to my car, then I got out and walked in the middle of them and we went in. Hen-C said, boy I haven't seen you since you were a little dude. I said C I need two of them. He said, bricks I shook my head up and down. Then I put the money on the table. His people started to count it, he told them that he knew my whole family. They don't need to count, then he asked how was Pat doing? I said he is ok, he said he hated to hear that about Sunny. I said that's Lil Sunny boy right there. He asked Sunny boy how was his mother and little sister doing. Sunny said, they're fine while he was talking the rental car was getting finished. Hen-C said that's a bad bitch right there. Then two cat's came in one of them shook his head up and down, I know they was counting that paper. They dropped a black bag on the table,

I had Everyday check it out. He said it was cool, then gave me the bag. I took my hat off, that was the sign to let Honey know to come knock on the door. Like clockwork she knocked on the door. Hen-C jumped up and opened the door. He said what's up pretty girl, she asked for change for a dollar. Before he could say anything I said that I do. She walked in and I gave it to her and on the way out she grabbed the bag and walked back out the door. Hen-C started to say something, I told him that's me play boy so lay on back. While we were talking she jumped in the rental, they opened the door and she went to the P.J's. We all walked out and jumped in the rides. Ten minutes later I had to show Hen that I wasn't a little boy in the game. We could have gave him the blues, and took his shit and his life it was that easy. Every day and Sunny boy didn't know she was there, you should have seen their faces when they seen Honey already in there. That was a smooth move there, now that was playa. When we made it back the car was in the lot. Sunny boy asked me, where is Honey playa? I told him to just play his spot.

He gave me a fucked up look, but he got back in pocket. When we all parked I told Everyday to wait till tonight to get the work. He said ok Rose, I called everyone to the front room. I told them tonight is the night, at one o'clock shop will open. The shifts will be from eleven to seven, seven to three, and three to eleven on the weekends. Slow said, damn twenty four seven on the weekends like seven eleven. I said the more time we put in at the start, the faster we can move up and put someone else in the house. Then go break another house in. do you feel me on that? They all said yeah.

Slow worked that voo doo and made two into four things. I had three of them broke down into twenties. On the street we call them rocks. I had three brick broke down in to rocks, one I took to pimp Sue in Iowa, we was putting the rape down like some pro's. I had Honey and Every day's girl making that trip dropping off and picking up. I must say my family was coming together.

Four months passed the game was lovely, money was coming in hand over hand. Pimp Sue was getting three bricks a month now I was still shaking Pat and his little chick. I haven't seen Velt in over five months. Me and Tarzan was seeing each other when he ran across them works. He would let me get them for a little bit of nothing. I was making a hundred thousand a week out of the projects. Nigga that live there was starting to have some problems with that. That's how cats are when they don't have any business skills. I know sooner or later it was coming, but they dumb ass let me get my money right for war.

I had a get together over my house, everyone came over. I sat everybody down and told them that this is was our last week in the projects. Everyday said what? Sunny boy, Jap, and Slow was just looking at me. Sunny boy said, Rose so we put in all that work just to give it to them? I said yeah, Jap said that's fucked up man Slow put his hands over his face. I asked Slow what did he think? He took his hands down from his face, then looked at me and smiled. He said Rosewood since I met you all of your moves have been good ones. I question some of them at the beginning, but you prove me wrong. We've been getting money playa, so I can only speak from me. Just tell me what you want me to do, and I'm behind you a hundred percent. The room was quiet when I looked over at Honey she had a smile on her face. As I looked in her eye's I already knew what she was thinking. I had the one I really needed in my corner, and that was Slow and my Voo doo man. Everyday said I'm in playa till the wheels fall off. Sunny boy looked at me and said you know what I do and that's all I have to say. Oh yeah and one more thing fuck all these soft ass nigga. They better back you or else I will back them. Then he pulled out his gun and put it on the table in front of him, and turned and looked at Jap. Jap said I'm in play boy.

Then I sat down and told them my new plan for the future of the family. I said that the cats in the jets are in there feelings about us getting that paper down there. I knew it was coming but it didn't, our money is right now it's time for us to move up, in this game that we are playing. I will pick a nigga from down there and put him in charge of business there. Everyday said, who do you have in mind? I said, Pee pee. Pee pee what about big bo? He said. I said that Big Bo would try to take over at the first chance he get he would try to knock one of us. Jap said that if you give it to Pee pee, Big bo is coming to press him. Everyday said, what made you say pee pee.

I said he washed my car one day I tried to give him fifty dollars he asked for fifty in dope. I told him to come to the shop later on that night. He did, I gave him the work. Three hours later he came back and bought two more. I paid a rock star to see what Pee Pee was doing. The star pulled back up on me and said, that Pee pee was making a sale for nine dollars or less. If they had ten or more he would send them to the shop. It's been five months Pee pee bought his first quarter bird a couple of weeks ago. Most cats I know would have tried to block the door. He saw a market and took it Slow said, that's why it was only twenty sales at the door. I'm glad they stopped coming for two dollar hits and shit like that.

I said that's why I want Pee pee to run the shop down there. He's a thinker he will get the work from us. Slow I want you to bring Pee pee in the shop, to show how the game go. This is our last week down here, don't tell him that. Everyday said what about Big Bo? I said FUCK BIG BO nigga! I will deal with Lil bo, I don't want to see you with lil bo either because when they come it's like that. If you are there I will send your people some money and flowers. Do you all understand? They all said yeah.

Then I had Honey call Velt to get Big Moon's number. She came back and called Big Moon. I told her to tell him that I would be down there this weekend and I'm looking to be loved. She said that he started laughing and said ok let's play. She hung up the phone.

When she came back in the room everyone was still there talking. She told me that it was on. I pulled her closer to me and kissed her on the cheek. Then I told her softly in her ear to go and book the tickets to Miami for Friday. She said how many? I told her two.

CHAPTER TWELVE

Rosewoods Close Call

The next day Velt called me up. I answered the phone, hello. Velt said, what's up play boy? I said, nothing playa is everything alright on your end? It's fine, why do you ask? He said. Because it's early for you to be on the move if it's not business. He said, man I have been thinking about you lately, I miss having you around talking shit with me. You don't come see me anymore. We don't play chess, shit we don't even play phone tag with a mother fucker. What have I done to you? I said Uncle Roosevelt it's not like that. He said, what the fuck is it like then, please tell me I would really like to know.

I said, I'm on my way over, ok? So have the board ready and tell Candy to cook some breakfast. Alright playa will that make you happy? Velt said, damn right a nigga shouldn't have to go through this to see his son. I said your son? He said come on over, then hung up the phone. I asked Honey did she want to go over Velt's house with me? She said yeah, we both got up and handled our business. When we got there I saw a car in the driveway that I had never seen before. I asked Honey had she ever seen it before, she said no. I parked and we got out, Honey knocked on the door then rang the door bell.

Jet answered the door smiling from ear to ear. I said, what's up blacker than me? she said, shit I thought you forgot where we lived. You being playa, playa and all I said girl go on somewhere with that bullshit. I see that ass still fat, she was walking away when I said that. She stopped and turned around, Honey told her, keep on walking bitch. Jet laughed and walked away. Now she was walking nasty like she was trying to pick up a trick off the street. I made my way to the living room, there was no one there but the board was set up. I told Honey to go get that weed out of the car. She said okay, when she came back in I made a honey blunt. I was there for about five minutes, blowing tripping off the years I spent in this house. I spent more time here than at Big mama's house.

I closed my eyes on the couch, when I heard a voice. What's up little nigga. I knew it wasn't Velt so I kept my eyes closed. Then I heard a woman say Pat, you hear me calling you boy. He said, what's up girl, candy wants to know if you want anything to eat, she said. He said yeah I really kept my eyes closed then. Honey walked in the kitchen and smacked Candy on the ass and said what's up old ho? Pat's little girlfriend was looking at Honey crazy as a motherfucker. I only met her once, that's when they came to town. Honey brought the keys to the house down, Pat's girl was tripping off her then, she thought Pat and Honey was messing around. Candy asked Honey has she ever met Tammy? Honey said, hi then turned her back on Tammy. Rosewood said put him a plate together. Candy said Rosewood in there girl? She said yeah.

Candy took off into the living room and said, Lil Rose get your fine ass up and give me a kiss. I opened my eyes stood up and gave her a hug. When I looked in the kitchen I saw Tammy standing in the doorway looking at me. Honey, Jet, and Tammy came in the living room. Pat said nigga I know you heard me? I said yeah I heard you. He said why didn't you say anything then? I knew you wasn't talking about shit, that's why I didn't say nothing to you nigga. Pat said, what little nigga! I said you heard me playa. Then I stepped up in his face, we were nose to nose.

I heard Velt say lil Rose let's play. Then he told Candy to go set the table, Pat said nigga I should have never put you on with your broke ass. Then he walked in the kitchen smiling with his girl behind him like a puppy. I called Honey in the living room, then I said Honey bring your ass in here now. I mean right now! I asked Velt to let me use the phone. He said yeah, but what's up Rosewood? Who are you calling? I told him don't trip. I called Everyday and told him to bring thirty gee's to the gas station fifteen minutes from him, and it was fifteen minutes from where we were. I told Honey to go get that for me, and top it off. She looked at me and hit the door. Roosevelt was looking at me, we finely made it to the board. He was whooping my ass too. Velt said, Rosewood what's up with your game? I said why didn't you tell me this nigga was over here man? He said I wasn't thinking about him, I just wanted to see you. What's up with you two anyway? I said Big Sunny died just like my father did. Fucking with Pat and some two dollar ass bitch. We wouldn't have had to move if it wasn't for Pat killing a cat over a bitch. Then my daddy killing a cat that saw Pat do that dumb ass shit. Man that nigga fucked up my life man. When we made that move out of town that was Sunny boy and me that put that nigga in that work on them cats. Now this nigga walking around like he heavy or something. Velt I love you man but fuck this nigga, Candy came in and told Velt that the food was ready. We got up and went in the dining room. We were eating for a minute when the door bell rang. It was Honey, when she came in the room she had the bag in her hand. She sat it down at the table right beside me. Pat and Tammy kept their eye's on me, I asked them what the fuck was they looking at? Tammy started to say something, Honey told her bitch he wasn't talking to you. Pat started to say something then I said bitch she wasn't talking to you.

Then Roosevelt said all of you shut the fuck up. The room got quiet, I had Honey hand me my black bag. I unzipped it, and stuck my hand in it and pulled out a nine mm and laid it on the table. Pat eye's got big and he slowly set back in his chair. I could see his chest moving faster and faster, the whole room was quiet. Tammy didn't say a mother fucking word. Then I went back in the bag, and grabbed thirty thousand and made sure I put it right in his food. I picked the nine up off the table and put it back in the bag. Then I told Pat, there you go heavy ass nigga. I wonder if you paid my old dude back when he put your broke ass on. I gave the bag back to Honey and she stood up and started to walk toward the car.

I got up and told Velt that we would holla when I came back for Miami. He said ok Rosewood, then I looked at Pat he was just looking at me in shock. See I was raised by Roosevelt and Tarzan in the street. We only seen Pat when he was in some shit, don't get me wrong I love my uncle but he knew how to carry me. When we left I dropped Honey off at the house and told her to pack, cause we leave tonight for Miami. She said ok and told me to be careful out there. I looked at her and told her that I loved her. It fucked me up I meant it too. I went to the projects, I was rolling to get my mind right. It was still early in the morning, the game was still sleep. I was passing a corner store when I saw Pee pee coming out of the store. I stopped and said what's up playa? Pee pee said, what's up Rosewood I'm trying to get where you at in this shit we call the game. I said that's what I want to holla at you about playa. Can I get a minute if your time play boy? Pee pee said damn right pimping.

He got in the car and the meeting was on. I asked him, would he like to get money with me in the game? I say it like that, because if you say work for me nigga in the street will feel like you are disrespecting them. They could be the brokest nigga in the world, and would still say no I'm cool play boy. But if you said get money with me, you are showing them respect and they are willing to share. You can't feel that's big business.

I told Pee Pee what I wanted to do with him, he was looking out of the window, he didn't say nothing for a minute then he asked me a question. Rosewood! I said what's up pimp? Pee Pee said the whole project, I said yeah, Pee Pee then said what about big Bo and his crew. I said I will handle lil Bo and his crew. Then I asked him what's up?

He was still looking out of the window, the whole time he was talking. Pee Pee was looking out of the window he turned toward me and was smiling from ear to ear. He said Damn right I'm in playa. I said welcome to the family my nigga. Pee Pee please don't ever forget I'm the top. He said I want Rosewood. I picked up the phone and called Everyday, I told him that Pee Pee was family now. I also told him to show him how we do it. Take him in the shop and, everything to do with that s okay. I'm out tonight and give me a week. He said, I will be through if not I will call from down there, he said alright playa.

I pulled back up and told Pee Pee that everyday will be at you. You got the number? Pee Pee said yeah, I got everyday's what's your? I said you got what you need play boy. He smiled and said Ok Rosewood. I mashed off, I called Sunny Boy on his car phone, he said hello, I said SB he said Wood what's up playa? I asked him where was he at? He told me he was at a car wash. I told him to hold, he said alright. When I pulled up, he was with two other cats. One was named Noses, and the other was named Vella. When I got out I gave Sunny Boy a hug. Then I kissed my cat on the cheek. He looked at me and said when, where, and who? I said that we will talk, a third nigga walked up and said Noses that BMW is tight we can take that from that mark ass nigga. My back was turned away from the dude, I'm looking at Sunny Boy, I reached and pulled out my nine, and turned around and put it under his chin. I made him get on his knees beside the car. Sunny Boy said, the police!! At this time I had the nigga on his knees the nine at his forehead. But from the view point of the police everything was normal.

We were just standing there getting our cars washed. I told the nigga that I was the mark ass nigga driving thee BMW. Sunny Boy said, he is with me Rosewood. Put it away man, I asked the nigga what was his name? He said buff, I put my nine up. Then I helped him get back on his feet. I told Sunny Boy to walk. I asked him them your cats? He said no they are your cats. Sunny Boy said what's up home boy? I said man I got so much shit on my mind right now. I got into it with Pat this morning. I'm up on him and checked his bitch, I gave him thirty gees for that brick that he gave me. Sunny Boy said, I thought that was a gift. I said me to pimping, But he was talking heavy and I snapped. Sunny asked, that ain't who you are talking about is it? I said no man, I'm talking about Big Bo and his crew. I need to know every move he makes. So if he trip we can touch him quick and fast. You feel me. He said I feel you pimping. I said before I forget Pee Pee is on the team now. Look out for him. Let nigga know he is family now.

I walked back over to the cats and told them you'll have to prove yourself to me. I see that. Then I jumped back in the BMW and mash off. I know that you are probably saying that I'm tripping today, trust me that I'm not. Those three guys are head knockers I have to show them that I get down also. I learned that from Tarzan, You get that out of the way before you get started with nigga's like that. So if they ever want to take over, they will always think, this nigga here Ain't no joke.

When the police rolled by it couldn't get no better than that. They saw no fear, I stayed claim, cool, and collected. I showed them that I was in control, and my eyes were on the prize. If that's not your trade, you wouldn't understand play boys and girls. When I made it back home all the bags was ready to go. I took a shower and got something to eat. Then I jumped in the bed for a couple of hours, we had three hours before we had to leave. My boo was from Miami so I had the best guide on my side. I had to rest this was an important trip, I had to be on my toes and on top of my game. This was my first move in business that didn't know my old dude. This is my tie here, this might be my life line. Like Denver to my old dude.

That couple of hours went by fast, it's time to get up and make that trip. On the way to the airport I called Roosevelt and told him its time. He started to talk about Pat, I told him man I'm going to Miami in a hour. That's important to me play boy. He said, "I understand playa. This is a business call. I said, this might be my life line in the game. He said, I understand. Pats life line was Tarzan, I said what. He was too scared to go get one. You are sixteen and Big Moon got the county on lock too. Don't forget he asked you so it just played out like that. He asked you to come down and holla at him. Do you feel me? I said damn right Velt, he said be yourself and play the game. And what's the game? Money I said, it's all about the paper. Roosevelt we at the air I'll holla. He said, make me proud. I said, I got you pimping and then I hung up.

It was about eleven o'clock when the plane took off the runway. Honey and I were in first class on our way to Miami. I told her, baby you know I only got about three months before i have to move back to St, Louis with my mother and little brother. Baby you was for real when you said that. I told her I gave my mother my word, she said fuck it I'm moving to Saint, Louis then. I said, that's my girl. She said I'm your bitch nigga, I have love for that too I said. We made it to Miami around three or three thirty in the morning. I was kind of restless too I guess Honey saw that because she asked me did I want to go out. I said, yeah why not, I had always heard of Miami night life. Now I'm here to see it for myself. We got booked into the hotel, than we hit the street.

We went to South Beach, it was live but I'm a person that takes note of everyone around me. When the vote came in, seventy percent of the crowd was guys, I asked Honey do you see what I see? She said what? I said the gay people, there hugging and kissing all over each other. Looked at them two over there they have braids and they doing the damn thing. Don't get me wrong if you like it I love it, and they partying up in here. She told me to come on and we jumped in the rental and went to a strip club. She said baby I use to work, I said all yeah. She said yeah, we walked in now this is my type of party. All I'm going to say is it was live. A couple of girls were trying to get on me. Honey came back and told them hoe's to step.

Then when the girl turned around Honey knew her. She said Kathy! Is that you? The girl just looked at Honey with her mouth open wide open. Honey started hugging the girl. I asked who is she an old friend or something. She said crying it's my sister my sister. I said shit I didn't know you had a sister. I asked Kathy when did she get off? She said in about an hour. I gave her the hotel address and told her to come on over. Then I tipped her, I gave her five hundred dollars and then told Honey to come on. When we got in the car I asked her why she didn't tell me she had a sister. She told me some shit that fucked me up. She said you never asked me about things like that. I had to sit back and draw off what she just said. I felt dirty as a mother fucker.

When we made it back to the hotel I took a shower. I had to get some sleep, I have a very important day ahead of me. When I woke up it was around ten o'clock, Honey and Kathy were sleep on the couch. Both of them are so beautiful, I ordered room service then I called Big moon. The meeting is set, they are coming to get me from the hotel in a half hour. I looked out of the window it was so beautiful. We were overlooking the ocean and the white sandy beach. I tripped off the buildings, they were all different colors loud colors but it seemed to work. I had the bell hop set the table up outside.

Let me tell u what was going on while I was out of town. Every day and Pee-wee hooked up. Every day showed him how to get down in the jects. Slow and jap was putting the word out on the street that pee-wee was on my team now. The street will put you all over the city in a day or too so now the streets' was watching pee-wee. Nigga in the game was showing him love. At the same time the nigga that didn't like us, now don't like pee-wee. Pee-wee found that out first hand when he was in the store and big bo pulled up on him. Big bo said, damn pee-wee homie, you fucking with soft ass nigga now. Pee-wee said yeah homeboy. I had to get down with that paper. Big Bo said nigga we from down here, them nigga Ain't. pee—wee replied, but they making all the paper. I know we are from down here but they got all the work. So I had to get in where I fit in, so my pockets can get right. Big Bo said nigga u better watch who you fucking with before you come up missing homeboy. Pee-wee just looked at big bo. Back in the day Big Bo used to beat up pee-wee and take his money. Pee-wee said, homeboy that's not for us, we can get this money together. Big Bo smiled and said, nigga I'm going to take over the jets. I'm working on it right now. I got a nigga lined up with the works. He don't like rosewood either. When it go down, you need to make a choice. The hood or the ho's. Big Bo made that move and left the store.

Pee-wee called Everyday and told him everything Big Bo had said. When I called home from Miami, Everyday told me the play. I told him to tell sunny boy, to do what I told him to do. He said okay and then we moved on to business. Everyday caught up to sunny boy. He told him what I said. Sunny boy and his crew was now in motion. The first thing they did was find Big Bo. When they did they called Everyday. Every day and I had a code set up. He would call me from a pay phone out in the streets. I would let my phone ring one time.

Then he would hang up and go back home. Thirty minutes later I would return the call from a pay phone in the streets of Miami. When I called back, he told me that they found Big Bo and sunny boy needed the word. I told him to watch, and find out who was fronting him that work. We need to catch them together. He said okay, and we both moved on in the game. Sunny boy followed that nigga. Now we know how many kids that nigga had. We even know where his late night hike was at. They was on that nigga for two days. Everyday had pee-wee call Big Bo. Pee-wee said Bo, I was thinking about what you was saying. About us being on the same team. You was right homeboy. The hood came before anything else. I need to comp a half a brick, what's good? Bo said I don't have that right now, I'm going to call my boy. Pee-wee said, call me if u can do it, if not I will l have to holla at Rosewood. Bo replied fuck Rosewood.

Sunny boy and the crew were outside. Big Bo came out, jumped in the ride and pulled off. Sunny boy and the crew were right behind him. This would make day three that they was on that nigga. If it was going to happen it needed to go down while I was out of town. They pulled up six blocks away from big mama's house. Then another car pulled up. Sunny boy didn't know the car, boy he knew the driver. When he noticed who it was he called Everyday right away. He told Everyday to get me on the three way asap. Everyday made the call. The phone was ringing and ringing. I step back in to answer the phone. It was Every day, he told me Sunny boy was on the phone, its important. I said what's up S.B? The connect is right in front of me. I said aww yeah. He said yeah. I told him to kiss his lil girl on both cheeks for me. S.B don't even have any kids. He said R.D? I said what. Sunny boy said the connect is Pat. I said okay.

This is what I need you to kiss that one. Real nice, I mean real nice. He said okay then. Then I told him to pass Pat the phone so I can talk to him. Sunny boy said, bet I can feel that. As they was sitting in the car talking business, Sunny boy, Norse, Buff and Vell pulled up on the car. The car Pat was in, Tammy was the driver. Buff had her at gun point with his hands over her mouth. Vell was on the driver side of the other car. Big BO was the driver. Sunny boy and Norse was on pat side. They were all masked up. Sunny boy told them to shut the fuck up. One sound and it's all over. He called Every day, I was still on the phone. Every day called back to Sunny boy so I could talk. I told S.B to give the phone to Pat. Hello. I said what's up uncle pat. He said, Rose? I said u knew me and Big Bo was at each other. Everybody in the street knew this. U wanted to help him get his crew stronger. Then you know the game. You knew when he got his money right, that he would be trying to kill me. I'm glad I'm a thinker playa, but check this out, I'll show you how I get down. Give the phone back to whoever you got it from. I love you man. Bye—bye play boy. I heard S.B voice back on the phone. I told him to hit that one right away. Remember the club. Reach across pat and do it. Before you leave show Pat your face and walk away. I got you. If he ever say anything about this I will touch him. That's my word. Sunny boy said okay, and he gave Every day the phone. I told Everyday that I would see him soon. Then I hung up the phone. Honey, Kathy and I went out to kick it. I had so much shit on my mind all I could do is get fucked up. Between me and you I don't know how I got back to the hotel last night. I know one thing, my head was banging. My last day in Miami, and I was in the bed with a hangover.

Later that night big Moon called me. He told me he was thinking about what we talked about. I said aw yeah, what's up? He said man I like you, and u kept it real with me. You are going to be alright Rosewood. You got a beautiful mouth piece too. I believe we will get a lot of money together. Did you enjoy your week in Miami? I said yeah it was cool, I will be coming back playa. He said, I'm ready when you are Rose. I said okay. Then I asked him would I have to come down. He said, no. I will bring it to you. I said that's cool. Then we hung up. Honey and her sister were having a ball. I never seen her this happy. I told her that she can come and stay anytime she wanted to. Then I gave her four thousand dollars. She said that she couldn't take it. I stood up looked down at her and smiled. Then I turned away and went into the other room to start packing. I heard her say to Honey, girl that nigga do what he wants to do don't he? She said yeah that's why I love him. He's good people. Then I closed the door and left them alone.

When I woke up the next day, she was gone. All the bags were packed and we was on our way home. My job was done. Now I was going to deal with the problem at home. On the trip home I was in my thoughts. I didn't say a word. Honey was doing all the talking. I was tripping off this shit with Pat. I hope I did the right thing by letting him know that it was us that put Bo down in front of him. I pray to god that this does not come back and bite me in my ass. When we made it home, I had Honey run me a hot bath. I must say it was nice to be back at home. Honey walked in and said, thank you. I said for what? She said you didn't have do that for my sister. I said that was from you not me. Then I asked her did she enjoy herself. She said baby u know I did.

I said that's cool then. She didn't know what happened with pat. I told her to call Roosevelt, and tell him that I was coming over tomorrow to talk about some business. She said ok then I smack her on her ass and she walked off. On the trip home I didn't say a word I was deep in thought. Honey was doing all the talking. I was thinking about the shit with Pat. As I looked out the window I found myself asking the question, I hope I did the right thing by letting him know that it was us that put down Bo in front of him. I pray to god that this doesn't come back to bite me in the ass.

When we made it home I had Honey make me a bath. I must say that it was nice to be home. Honey walked back into the room and said thank you. I looked at her and said, thanks for what? She looked at me and smiled, then told me that I didn't have to do that for her sister. I told her that was from you not me. Then I asked her did she enjoy herself. She said baby you know I did. As I walked away I told her that was cool. She doesn't know what happen to pat yet. I told her to call Velt and tell him that I was coming over tomorrow to talk about some business. She said ok then I smacked her on her ass as she walked out the room.

When I got up the next day I called over to Velt house. I told him that I would be over there around one o'clock. He said ok then told me to come by myself. I told him ok see you later then I hung up the phone. When I set down in my chair I was tripping off him telling me to come by myself. Velt was my second father. I said to myself shit he wants to talk to me by myself. I was kind of shock that he was so laid back on the phone. Then I thought about it Pat just might not have said nothing about it.

The time came and I was right on time like always. When I pulled up I saw Tarzan's car and Pat's in the driveway. When I made it to the door Tarzan opened the door for me. I wasn't use to that. I was use to Candy and jet answering the door here. When I walked in I heard voices coming from the den. So that was where I went too. The den is where Velt handle his business at. It was kind of like the god fathers den but he had a round oak wood table with tall back chairs. All four walls were cover with book shelf. When I walked in I saw Pat setting next too Velt and Tarzan set on the other side. We were the only four people in the house. As I set down at the table the meeting began. Velt started off by asking me how was my trip? I told him that it was lovely and the game was fair to me. he smiled and said, that was good. I could feel the shit in the air. So I turned to Pat and asked him why the fuck was he fucking with Bo? You knew he wanted to knock me out the game! Pat looked away and started to say that he didn't know.

Tarzan stood up and cut Pat off and said, Bullshit!!! The hole city knew the play on them two niggas there. That's how I knew what the fuck was going on. So I can't believe that shit there! Velt told Tarzan to sit and claim down. Then he asked me what happen? I told him the plan was to knock Bo out the box when I was in Miami. So I had my boy's watch his every move. I wanted them to wait until he was getting a pack. So I had one of my guys put in a order with him. The goal was to knock and grab. Then to every one's delight this nigga Pat is the one putting this nigga on. I was trying to kill two birds with one stone. When I got the call and they said that Pat was the other mark. I had to change the plain a little bite. I was getting my dick suck and that news there fucked my mood up.

Then I thought back to when Pat tried to carry me like a bitch ass nigga the last time I was in front of his bitch. I had to make a point then. So I know you know the rest of the story from there. Tarzan told Pat I heard how you tried to do lil rose in front of your bitch. I should get up and walk around this table and smack the shit out of you! We have been dealing with this shit here for too long. I feel where Lil rose is coming from. This is the same man that handle, your business when yo puck ass got shot and that's how you thank him? I wouldn't fuck with yo ass either. I would have still took your dope! Might have told my guy to hit, your ass too.

Then Pat asked me why didn't I fuck with him when he came home? I looked at him and said, I was tripping off Sunny boy lost his dad over some bitch you were fucking with. My father would have never left Detroit if it wasn't for you fucking with some bitch. So I told myself that I wasn't going to die fucking with you and some bitch. I told him that he was on his own when it comes to shit like that. He sat back in his chair he didn't say a word. he was just looking at me. velt looked at Pat and said, you were wrong Lil bro. Then he looked at me and said that I handle that shit like a playa and he took his hat off to me on my move.

Then he asked me what was my plain's for the future? I looked at him and said the future? He smiled and said that I only have a couple of months before you move back to St. Louis with your mom. I shook my head and said man I don't know if I can do that. Rosevelt stood up and said Rosewood you gave her your word. Then I asked him to give me a week to think about everything. He said ok. Velt asked Pat if he had anything to add? Pat stood up and said Rosewood can you find it in your heart to forgive me man? I told him that I always had love for him. You just didn't want to give me my respect I was asking for. I guess now I can stand in my father shoes as a man.

A week has pasted all four of us are back at the round table again. I called this meeting here so the floor is mind. I told them that my plain was to move back too St. Louis to get to know my mom and Lil brother again. Then I turned to Pat and asked him if he would like to run my family? First he had a fucked up look on his face. Then after I told him that it was still mine I needed him to oversee it for a minute he Ok. I told Velt that I was thinking about making a move in ST. Louis. Then I told Pat that I wanted my team to stay the same don't bring in none of your guys or shit like that and you must treat them like men. Everyday will still run my show. I need you to keep that work in his hand and get my cut. Then I asked Velt to watch Pat and make sure he do me right. Pat then asked me if I had a connect, I said yeah. then I asked him how many he had left? He told me that he had seven bricks left. I told him to let me have them.

Then I asked him to let me get three for the deal between you and I. That's all me there you won't see a dime from that. The other four I will pay the going rate for. He didn't say anything for a minute. Then Velt told him that he couldn't bet that with a bat playboy. Pat looked around and said ok. I told him that I had to have that three up front a.s.a.p. I did it like that so I could make some money. Some real money, because I haven't been in ST. Louis in years when I get there I will have to see who the player's are. Then I would love to just watch from the sideline for a change. Then I told Pat one more thing Pimp Sue is all me playboy, he said ok. Then I called my crew and told them to meet me over Everyday house. When I got there I told them what was going on. I told them all the spots they had to play and said that from time to time I would meet them to see how everything was going on. I told Sunny boy to come on up and holla at me. When he made it up stairs I told him that if I needed him that he was still my right hand man. You will only deal with me, he said ok boss. I told him that he was my eye's and ear's in the family. He looked at me and said that he understood the move then he hug me and gave me a kiss on my cheek.

Them two months went by so fast now it was the end of the summer. Velt gave me a going away party. We were all there it was a sad party if I may say so myself. When I made it back home Honey was looking like a sad puppy. I told her that I was going to send for her in a month to six weeks. I told her to move back in with Velt we already talked about it. Then she asked me about this place? I told sunny boy to take the note over and she started crying. I pulled her close to me and began rubbing her pretty long hair and told her that I love her so much with all my heart.

The next day she took me to the airport that was the longest walk I ever took in my life. Detroit was my city now, this is how my father had to feel when he left. I told Honey that I loved her and turned around and walked away towards my new life. Before I stepped on the plain I turned around and she was still there beautiful as ever crying. It was so hard to stand by my word this day here. They called over the intercom last call from Detroit to ST. Louis. I said good bye to Detroit.

CHAPTER THIRTEEN

Rosewood Return

When I was on the plane a lot of things went through my mind. Things like where would I, fit in at my mom's house. Will she still try to treat me like a little boy? Will I get alone with her so call man or what? Will she try to put me back off in school? How is the neighbor hood? What's up with my people scrap? What's up with my little brother will we get alone after all these years? I guess you can see that I had a lot of shit on my mind.

As I walked off the plain I saw my mother and my little brother. My mother told him there he go Alex! She was smiling from ear to ear. She gave me a big huge then I picked up my little brother. When I put him down I told him that he got big on me and he grab my leg. I couldn't do nothing but smile. I heard a voice say come on baby. I looked around it was her man. She told him that I was her oldest son lil rose. He said what's up little guy. Then he stuck his hand out and said that his name was mike. I shook his hand and told him that my name was Rosewood. He looked at me and smiled. My mother looked at me and asked if I had any other bags? I told her no the rest would be here in a month or so. Mike asked me if I wanted him to carry my bags? I said no I was cool, but thanks any way.

When we made it to the parking lot Mike pulled up in a old ass van. I asked my mother how was she doing? She looked at me and smiled, she said baby we are fine then I got into the van. When we hit the highway I was looking out the window. The city looked funny to me. Every time I looked up Mike was looking at me kind of crazy in the rearview mirror. In my mind he was just checking me out. Him and my mom been together for some time now. To him it was only the three of them. Now here I come and I'm sixteen years old. Shit by the way the van look, they not doing so well. When we got off the highway we got off on Adelaide exit. That's on the north side of town. I asked my mother did Scrap still live on the north side of town. She told me that they only lived a few blocks away. That brought a smile to my face. When we pulled up to the house I was like dam my mom is living in a shack. I looked at my little brother his little eyes lit up and he said home.

When we got out of the van and went into the house. It was messed up okay. It was clean and I have seen worst. My mother then showed me to my room where I shared with Alex. The little house was a two bed room starter home. When I came out of my room I asked her for scrap phone number. I called and he answered the phone. Hello, I said what's up lil pimping. All I could hear was who is this? I said Rosewood! He said, who? I said Lil Rose nigga! I could hear him smiling on the phone. He asked me where I was at? I told him that I was at my mama's house. He said shit I'm on my way! I smiled and said cool play boy come right now. When I hung the phone up I called Velt back in the Dee.

When I looked up mike was watching me. I heard that sweet voice said hello, it was Honey. I smile and said I love you boo. She started crying telling me that she miss me.

I told her that I missed her to. Then I asked her to please put Velt on the phone real quick. She asked me was I ok? I said yeah baby I'm fine. She handed the phone to Velt. The first thing out his mouth was did I like it? I told him that it wasn't home. Then I asked him about Pat and my business? He told me that everything was cool on his end. I asked him to make sure Honey stay on top of my paper. He said ok pimping. Then asked me when was I sending for Honey? I told him at the first of the month. He said ok then put Honey on the phone. We talked about an hour. I heard the door bell ring.

When Mike opened the door Scrap was standing there. I told Honey that I would call her back in a couple of days and hung up the phone. Scrap walked over and gave me a huge. He told me that he was glad to see me. I told him that it has been too long. Mike asked me who I was talking to on the phone I looked at him and said that I was handling some business back in Detroit. He stepped up and said that he pay the phone bill round here. I said so then turned back around to talk to Scrap. He walked off and went and told my mother something. When she came in the room she started in on me about the phone. I looked at him and he smiled.

Then I asked him if he paid the phone? He said yeah. Then I reach into my pocket and pulled out a hundred dollar bill and put it right beside the phone. Then I picked it up and called pimp sue in Iowa and gave him the number to my mama's house. Then I told Mike that I would be calling back to Detroit tomorrow to handle some business.

Then I asked him if that would cover me are did I need more? He couldn't say shit I wish you could have seen his mother fucking face. Scrap looked at me and said that it took me long enough for me to come back home. I smile and told him that I was a Dee boy know. The look on his face changed. I told him to come back to my room. When we walked in we both set on the end of my little bed. I asked him what was his game He asked me what kind of game? Then I asked him how do you get paid? He told me that his mother give him money every two weeks. I started to smile then asked him how much did he get every two weeks? He told me twenty dollars. I said nigga that's no money then I asked him how much money he had on him right now? He said not a dime. Then I reach into my pocket and pulled out a knot.

Then the door opened up!!!! It was Mike standing there looking at us. He walked over and grab for my money. He called my mama into the room. When she walked in he started telling her about all this money I had in my hand. This cat here was crazy. He told me to give him my money. I told him that he was crazy. Then he reached his hand out to take my money. I pulled away from him. Then my momma told me to give her the money. I stopped and looked at her crazy too. Then I asked her why should I? Do you need some? She said yeah., just let me hold it for you. I told her that I would give her some, but I can hold my own. I had five thousand and gave her twenty five hundred. Then I walked back over to the phone and took back that hundred I give Mike. Scrap and I walked out of the house. We were on the front when Scrap said dam cuzz what's your game? I said a D-boy. For ones that don't know a D-boy is a person who sales drugs. Then I gave Scrap two hundred dollars. Then I told him that it would get greater later. We spent the rest of the night talking about old times. Then I put him up on what we needed for the future. Three weeks has passed and the Mike has been on my hills since I been here. I have met a few nigga's from the hood. My nigga Holly bird was from the south side of town. I must say that nigga there is a real player in the game. He's moving that shit for real in the streets. As I set on the sideline I'm starting to feel the grip. The grip is when a fin needs to get high. It's no different for a playa that gets money in the street. Shit I start school tomorrow I have missed three weeks already. The name of the high school is Beaumont high school. to the people in the street they call it c-mont. They call it that because the crips run the school. When I walked into the school, the first thing I saw was the guards and metal detectors. Damn near every boy and girl had on blue. I had on polo from head to toe. People was looking at me kind of crazy. They didn't sell Ralph Lauren in St. Louis yet. As I saw the kids moving through the hallway, I noticed something. The gang was running the trade in the school. When I went to the bathroom between classes there were more dudes moving more dope then in the neighborhood. They even had guards on their team, but the hardest gang in the school was Adelaide Ave. When I went to lunch they were all sitting together. They called me over to their table. I sat down. I knew all of them from the hood. Petty was a small guy, but he was about paper. He had his house rocking. I know if he had more product, sky would be the limit for him. To my right was short dog T. He was also a little guy, but he had all of heart though. I saw him as someone who would handle their business on site. There were a lot more at the table, but the two I told you about was the ones I use to watch a lot in the hood.

Another two weeks passed. This nigga Mike was really riding me around the house. He was treating me less than a man. I found myself biting my tongue a lot. When I talked to my mother about it, she would tell me how good he is. I pulled Mike to the side one day. I asked him why was he on me like he was? He told me that I didn't respect him or my mother. He had to remind me that I was a child, and that little money I had was going to run out soon. Then I was going to be asking him to take care of me. I told him, nigga you can barley take care of yourself. Aw he was hot. He told me, as long as I stay under his roof I would do what the fuck he said. My mother heard the last part of the conversation, when she walked into the room. I told him that it was time he meet the real me. As I walked out the room, I could hear my mother telling Mike that I wasn't a regular kid like that. That boy is grown. That's what's wrong with him. Now he thinks he grown.

While they were talking, I was on the phone purchasing a one way ticket back to the Dee. It was Friday. I could make it back by Sunday night or Monday. I called my mother into the front room. I asked her to take me to the airport, she asked me why? I told her that I was going back to Detroit. She asked me for what? I told her that I was home sick. She said that this is your home. I replied, this is Mike's home. Two men can't live together, I must leave. She started to cry. I told her that I would be back Sunday, no later than Monday. Mike said that I wasn't going anywhere. I looked at him. Then I told my mother that if she loves him, tell him not to touch me. Either you take me to the airport or I will walk outside and call a cab. He started to open his mouth and walk towards me. My mother told me to get my bags. I told her that I didn't need any. She took Mike's keys, and drove me to the airport.

She was talking about Mike the whole way. I told her that I didn't mean any disrespect, but I didn't want to hear about her man anymore. When we got to the gate, I stop to call Velt on the pay phone. I heard a sweet voice say, hello. It was Honey, I said let me talk to Velt. She said, Rose. I said, yeah baby it's me, put Velt on the phone right away. I could hear her moving through the house real fast. I could hear her tell Velt that something was wrong with me, and I wanted him on the phone. Velt picked up the phone and said, yeah baby boy! I told him to pick me up at the airport at 1:30 gate 3D. Then I said tell Honey to come get me. He asked me what was up. I told him that I would speak on it in person. Then I hung up the phone.

When I got off the phone the first person I saw was Honey. She was looking sexy as ever. I walked up to her and gave her a long hug. She said damn baby you missed me for real didn't you! I told her that she didn't know the half of it. She reached around me and put her hands into my back pocket. I felt a knot in my pants, it was five g's. I knew then that I was back at home. When I pulled in the driveway, it felt so good to see Velt's house again. I was smiling from ear to ear, deep down I was missing my little brother though. When I opened the door Jet gave me a big hug. Then Candy smacked me on my ass and said, welcome home Rose. Velt was sitting in the den. He called me, Rosewood! What's the deal lil pimping? I came in and set across from him.

I started off by telling him that Mike and I wasn't getting along. He said that he told my mother that it wasn't going to work out like that. He also said that Mike was going to try to prove a point. That he was the man of the house. Then he asked me how my mother was doing? I told him that she was the middle man all the time. I really don't like her being in the middle of all this shit. I told Velt that it's time for me to get my own place. I really think Mike and I would get along then. He said playa, you know two men can't live together without understanding. I told him that I tried to get some understanding. The man not trying to hear shit I say. Velt stated, that man sees you as a child. He doesn't know anything about the life we live. He's a lame to the game. Your mother picked a lame. She doesn't want to go through that shit again, like she did with your father. You can't blame her.

I told Velt that I could understand that. I would give Mike his respect as a man. Velt told me that was pimping there playa. I told Velt that I would talk to him in the morning. He said ok, then I walked upstairs to Honey room. When I opened the door, she was in something real sweet. She told me to come to bed, her bed has been cold for too long.

When we got up the next morning I had some business to deal with. Honey and I got ourselves together and hit the streets. My first stop was Everyday's house. When I got there he buzzed me up. When Honey and I walked in I gave her that look. She took Everyday girlfriend into the bedroom. Now Everyday and I was alone. He asked me how was St. Louis? I told him that I was going to set up shop there. He said, for real. I just looked at him. Then I asked him about Pat and the business? He started smiling and said that the project is on line in a major way. I said that's good, what's up with Sunny Boy?

He said, shit, everything is slow. We have no problems with anyone. I told him that I was only in town for a day. I called Honey into the room. When she appeared I instructed her to call Pat. She replied, okay daddy, then she walked out the door. I told Everyday that I would see him again before I leave. Then I gave him a hug and told him to be safe.

I met Honey at the car. She was returning from the pay phone up the street. When I handle my business I only mess with phones that are planted into the land. She told me that he was waiting on me. we jumped in the car and headed to Pat's house. When we got there his girlfriend was on the front. Honey knew the play already. As soon as the car stopped, Honey asked her to come and ride with her to the store. She told Honey to hold on she was coming. She walked past me and said, hello. I said hi back then walked into the house. Pat was sitting in the kitchen cooking some food. I was like what's up pimping/ he was like same ole same ole play boy. He gave me a hug then he said, damn you checking up on me already nephew. I told him that it wasn't even like that. I came to town to get Honey, my whips, some money and work. He looked at me and said, some work? I told him that it was all good in the lou. I had to do something for Pimp Sue this month anyway.

I asked him was everything cool? He replied, shit like clockwork play boy. I pulled me a chair up to the table then put my face in my hands. Pat looked at me and asked, what's wrong lil pimping? I told him that I found myself missing my old dude. In my heart I know that this is not the life he wanted for me. now I was hooked to the rush of the streets. He looked at me and said, baby boy I see your father in you more than you think. He told me to hold on then walked off to the back room. When he came back he gave me four keys of dope and seventy thousand dollars. I called Honey on the car phone and told her to call me a cab from a pay phone and send it to Pat's house. She said okay, then she said, I'm on my way back. I told her to come right now. She made it back about ten minutes before the cab did. I gave her the bag with the dope and money. I jumped in the BMW and trailed. The game is in full effect. I have this shit" Pimping". We always play it like that, because if the law stop me, Honey and the package will make it through. The whole thing is to make it through. We made it back to Velt's house and laid low until Sunday night. We had over one hundred and seventy thousand dollars to go to St Louis with. We had both cars packed and ready to go. Velt told me to be careful and gave me a kiss.

CHAPTER FOURTEEN

The Take Over

We made it back to ST. LOUIS Monday after noon. We got a room down town at the Holiday inn. Honey had a look on her face that I never saw before. When we check in I asked her what was wrong? She said nothing. Then she looked at me and said that this was the first time she has been in ST. LOUIS in the day time. I looked at her crazy. Then she told me to stop looking at her crazy like that. Then she told me that the only time she has been here was the night they came and get me. The night of the playas ball.

I asked her what went down at the playa ball? She told me everything that she knew. She got up and walked from the bed towards the mirror. She was looking into the mirror as she talked to me. She said shit who knew that I was coming to get the only man I have ever loved that night. When she lifted her head there was a tear rolling down her cheek. I got up off the bed and walked up behind her and put my arms around her waist. I kissed her on her neck. Then I looked her in her eyes in the mirror. Then I told her that I loved her with everything I have in my heart. She turn around and told me that she has never been on her own before. Roosevelt made it happen, now it's you and I to count on each other. I set her down and told her, baby I had to come back and get my better half. She looked up at me and asked me is that how u felt about me? I said dam right! Now it's time to put the game in play. I picked the phone up and called my mother's house. Mike picked up the phone and said hello. I told him that it was me lil Rose and I needed to talk to my mother. He told me that my mother and I were worried about me. Then he asked me where was I? I told him that I was down town at the holiday inn down town. Then he asked me why I didn't come home? I told him that we would do better in our own homes. He laughed and said Rose you are only sixteen years old you can't get no house! I told him that I had my woman livening with me down here. He asked me if my mama let her come down here. I told him to put my mama on the phone.

Hello I heard her voice, mama it's me lil Rose. She said boy where the fuck you been! I told her that I was at the hotel down town. Then she asked me why didn't I come home? Then I told her that I was coming over in about an hour or two. Then she asked me if I needed a ride? I told her that I was cool. Then I heard mike off in the back ground saying that he got his girl friend with him. She said boy you brought a girl down here! I told her that I would talk to her when I come over. Then I hung the phone up.

I told Honey to come on and we jumped off into the B.M.W on them gold Dayton wheels. It was a beautiful day outside. I stopped at a pay phone and called pimp sue up. I told him that he had to come to ST. LOUIS to pick up. He told me that he would call me when he hit town. The last thing I said was pimping I'm ready then hung the phone up. I jumped back in the car. I must say that Honey was looking so sexy.

I picked up the phone and called Scrap. I told him that I was on my way to pick him up. He said ya nigga in what? I started to smile and said yeah you just don't know playboy. As I rolled down West Florssaint that candy paint was shining. It looked so wet and that tan interior on them gold Dayton rims and the music was bumping. There are only a few people who know how this feels. It's a beautiful feeling. I got the sun roof open the sun is nice and bright. When people saw the car they would look at it all the way down the street. I could see their eyes light up like dam he's doing it.

When we pulled up in front of Scrap's house he was out there with Petty, Nosey, Tuna and C.L. I pulled over and parked. Honey got out of the car and walked around the back of it, and open my door. I got out and walked up to them and told Scrap to go get in the backset. When I got back in the car I turned the music up and pulled off. We went to northwest plaza to the mall and went shopping. We spent about thirty two hundred. On Honey, scrap and some things for my little brother. When we pulled up in front of my mother's house my little brother was in the yard playing. Mike was outside watching my little brother Alex. My mother heard the music and came outside of the house. Honey got out of the car and walked around the back of the car and opened my door. Scrap got out of the back sit of the car on the passenger side. Mike still had his eyes on Honey. When Scrap got out he looked surprised. I guess because there were some neighborhood dealers across the street. In the hood we call them super stars.

Then I stepped out of the car. I had on a pair of blue guess shorts, a fitted tank top tee shirt, with a white thick tee shirt over the tank top. I also had a blue bee bop ferry kango hat and some blue cartaz Nikes. Street name dope man nikies with some knee high socks. When we were at the mall I bought a gold chain with a loin head on it. The loin eyes were diamonds. When I got out the car my little brother run up to me and gave me a hug. My mother told me that she was glad to see me back. She also said that she thought I wasn't coming back. I looked at her and told her that I gave her my word. Mike was now sitting down in a chair on the front porch. I grab my mother's hand and walked her up to Honey and she said hello. My mother looked at her and said hi baby we have met before. I thought you two had something going on. Honey started to smile. Then she told me that Honey was a beautiful young woman. Then she told Honey to take care of her baby. Honey told her that was the plan.

Mike stood up and walked over towards us my mother told her that this was her man mike. Honey looked over at me. I licked my lips then she shook his hand. I told Scrap to get them clothes out of the trunk. We all went into the house were my mother had made a nice dinner for us. Scrap mother called down to the house and told Scrap to come home because it was getting late. He asked me if I was going to school tomorrow? I told him yeah. Then I told him that I will be there to pick u up around 7:30 am ok. He looked at me and said make it 6:30 then he left. Mike kick it off and asked me where was I going to stay at? I told him that I was paid up at the hotel for the next two weeks. My mother looked at me and said, baby you can't stay in no hotel. Honey told her that's until we find a place. Mike then asked Honey where did she plan on living at?

She told him anywhere Rose would like to live. Then I told mike that I saw some apartments for rent across the highway from the arch. Mike looked at me and asked do you know how much a one bed room cast? I said no. He didn't have a problem telling me. I could see it in his eyes he was about to enjoy this one. He told me that it was three hundred and ninety five dollars for a one bed room, then you need first and last month rent. I sat there and added it up in my head. I looked at Honey and told her that it was one thousand eight five dollars. She told me that she would get right on it in the morning. I told her that I loved her. Then I asked my mother if she would go with her down there tomorrow. Before she could say anything mike jumped in and said that I have to take the van to work tomorrow! I told him that was ok Honey can drive her own car. Then he asked me how was I getting to school tomorrow? I told him that I was planning on driving my own car. He then asked me what other car? My mother jumped back in and said that she didn't have a problems with that. I told her thanks and that I loved her. Then I told her that I had to go to sleep so I can get up in the morning. She asked me to come through in the morning before you pick Scrap up. I told her that was no problem for me to do. So we left. When we got back into the car Honey said that mike was a trip. I told her to pay attention so you can get back tomorrow. She looked at me and said don't I always? I said yes you do smart ass. She started smiling and said that's why you love me. I couldn't disagree with her. I also showed her where the apartments at too.

The next morning came. I was up and early. I kissed Honey on the cheek and jumped into the shower. I loved hitting the street, when the playas in the game are sleep. I jumped into my Eloc it was midnight blue with dark blue tent on some chrome Dayton rims. It also had a three fifty motor in it. I must say that it sound so good when I use to jump down on it. I made it around six o'clock in front of my mom's house. I called her on my car phone I didn't won't any problems with mike this morning. When she answered the phone I told her that I was out side. I heard mike in the back ground asking her who was that on the phone. She told me to come in. I asked her if she would come outside to the car so we could talk. She said ok then hung the phone up.

When she came out and got into the car and said, baby you are just like your daddy. You like pretty cars and fast money. Baby we didn't won't this life for you. I wanted you to come back here to get away from that shit. Then she told me that I was moving too fast. I know what ever I say to you. You are going to do your own thing. Let me tell you this I want you to keep that shit from around my house and my baby. I don't want no dirty money from you. You understand me?

I told her that I understood her. Then I asked her if she was still going down town with Honey today? She looked at me and said baby I know you need some where to live. I saw the door open and it was mike standing there looking at us from the door way. I told her that her man was looking for her and laughed. She told me to be quite boy and got out of the car. I told her that I loved her. She just looked at me and then she closed the door.

I couldn't do nothing but respect her wishes. I pulled off to pick Scrap for school. It's kind of hard to know that your mother don't respect the man you have become. Three weeks has passed Honey is in love with her new life in ST. LOUIS. It was time to put that work on the street. I beeped Petty and he called me right back and asked me who was this? I told him that it was Rose wood. He said what's up play boy? I told him you. Then I asked him where was he at? He told me O'fallon park. Then I told him that I was coming thru there in about ten minutes. He said ok I'll be waiting. Then I told him that it was time play boy. When I pulled up Petty was sitting on the bench. C.L was over by the swing set. After I parked Nosey, Tuna, and Pack dogg pulled up behind me. We had all got cool in the neighbor hood and at school. We all grab a spot on and around the bench. My first question was who want to get some money? See I was thought that there is one topic of conversation that can get you five minutes with anyone in the world. From the riches to the poor's man in the word. When you talk about money every one will stop what they are doing to listen.

Every one said, shit who don't want to make money. I asked one more question. Do you believe in team work? They all looked at me kind of crazy. C.L said what kind of team work. I said, the kind of team work where everyone has their own spot, or for a better word, position. One man can't do it all by himself. He actually could, but his money would come slow. Then Petty said, slow money is for sure money. I told him your right if your moving an ounce. You have to move a lot different moving thirty-six ounces at a time.

I heard Nosey say, that's fast and reckless money. I could see his eyes light up. I always liked that nigga style. Nosey was a lil guy but he had big heart. He reminded me of Sunny Boy, but he had a lot of energy. Pack dogg said, I can understand where you coming from about the team. If everyone masters their position, there is a lesser chance to fuck up as a team. Pac dogg was about six five. He was real laid back, but could snap out at any given moment. He was one of them guys you would hate to see on the other team. That's why I must have him on my team. Then tuna said, shit if everyone play their own position, they would stay out of everyone else's mother fucking way. Tuna was a cool cat. If we are laid back, he is laid back. If we are tripping, then he is tripping. He was down for whatever, whenever.

I took back over the conversation. The plan is to get this money. I need to know how the market is ran. Petty asked, the market? I said from rocks to weight is the product. The user is the customer. The sales of the product to the customer in a place where product is offered for sale, or the process of buying and selling a particular type of product is the market. Petty said, okay I get it. Well we sell a rock for twenty bucks. We don't take no shorts on our block. That's how everyone do it down here. I said, what that's how it's going down? He said, yeah it's popping. I sat back for a minute thinking about a way to muscle my way in the game. I asked them another question. What if we offer the customers two rocks for the thirty and four rocks for the fifty? C.L said, man u crazy! Shit two rocks costs forty dollars all day long, and four rocks is eighty. Shit we will lose money. I asked, why would you lost money. He said everybody and their mama will be on the block.

I said bingo, that's what I'm talking about. We couldn't keep enough on the street. I told them I got that. My position is to keep it in your hands. Your position is to move the product and get money. Nosey and Pack dogg looked at each other and said mother fuckers in the city will be trying to take us out the game. I said you know why! They said, why? I replied, we would rule the city. When the other guys realize what's going on, we will be on top. We will be too strong by then. Tuna said, shit play boy you know that business shit don't you. I told him that their only two differences between a legal and illegal business. One is the product and two is the taxes. Petty asked me about the guys that wanted to buy some weight. I told him that the deal four for fifty is for the user and the seller. The seller can see that thirty dollar profit. My beeper went off. Listen up guys, am I making any sense? They all said yeah. Do you want to be in my family? They all said dam right, one by one. I told them that I would be coming to petty's house later on. I told petty to come on and ride with me.

Petty and I jumped in the elco. While we were pulling off I called Honey from the car phone. She was the one beeping me. She picked up the phone. Hello, what's up, baby you alright. She said yeah, I was thinking about you. I told her to find an outside line, it's important. She said okay, Then hung up the phone. Petty and I were rapping about the game. I told him that I was looking for someone to be my right hand man. I told him that he had the same kind of attitude for this type of position. I have been watching you since I been here.

My phone rang. When I answered, it was Honey. She gave me my phone number. I told her that I would call her right back. I pulled over and jumped on the first pay phone. I called Honey right back. I told her to grab four ounces and I will roll by the parking lot. I wanted her to trail me to the drop off spot. She said I will beep you when I'm ready. She said don't call back, I will be in the car on the lot. I said okay and then hung up the phone.

When I got back in the car I asked petty did he have a scale, He said no so we went to the store and bought a digital sale. As we got back in the car, my beeper went off. The cod read #001. It was Honey. When I was two minutes out I beeped her and hit my code, and put two on the end of it. When I rolled by I saw her. She put three cars between us. When we got to petty's house, I got out the car and stood on his porch. Then she hit the corner. Petty looked at me when she pulled up. I went to the car to grab the bag. Then I told her to meet me at home. I told her we were going to the movies and shopping today. She like that. I spent about two hours with petty bagging up four ounces to fifty packs. I told him how much to put on the set. I told them, tonight would change our lives. When the word gets out, it's like that. Two years had passed. The game was on and popping. The money was coming hand over fist. My team in ST. Louis was strong and moving like a well oiled machine. Playas in the game didn't know what hit them. Money was drying up in the other neighborhoods. The only other guys keeping up with us was a hustler named Lil Jimmy. He was from a hood that was a couple of blocks over. I guess you can say that he was my competition. I had some words with him one night at the club.

He pulled up on Honey and tried to talk to her. She told that nigga that she was in a fruitful relationship and smiled at him. Then she turned around and walked away from him back towards me. He grab her arm and turned her back towards him. He told her that he knew who the fuck her man was. Then he told her that his name was Lil Jimmy and he run this mother fucking city. Ho go and tell your man that. Honey threw her drink in his face and he let her go. She started walking towards our table and Nosey saw what happen and took off towards the bar.

I stayed off in the booth with Pack dogg and C.L. jimmy grabbed her again this time he was trying to put his hands on her. When Nosey pulled up behind her I saw what was going on Pack dogg, C.L and myself came down there. I saw Nosey tell Lil Jimmy if you put your hands on her that will be the last person you will ever touch on earth! He was looking all crazy when we walked up. He was afraid of Nosey. I asked him what was going on with you and my bitch? Now we were standing toe to toe nose to nose. Honey started to talk. I reached back behind me and touched her leg. At the same time I kept my eyes on Lil Jimmy punk ass. When I touch her she stopped talking and shit got quite.

Jimmy started off say that this city wasn't big enough for the both of us. I started smiling and moving backwards towards our table. When we got to our table I told Honey to grab our things. I told everyone to come on we were leaving. Nosey, Pack dogg, C.L and Petty was looking at me crazy. We were on our way out when we saw Scrap on his way in. I pulled up on him and told him that there was a change of planes. We were having his going away party at my house.

See when I made my move to play in ST. LOUIS I didn't include Scrap. I wanted him to make up his own mind up on his life, but I always looked out for him. When I shopped he shopped. When I ate he ate. One day he came in and said that he signed up for the army. I thought he was playing then he showed me his paper work. Three weeks later he was shipping out in the morning. That's why I was at the club. So we all grabbed all our women and went to my house. I could feel my guys I knew they wanted to know why we didn't get it on in the club. As soon as I walked through the door I heard Nosey say, Rosewood what happen man?

I told everyone to sit down then I answered his question. I was taught that a business man must always watch his actions in public. Then if anything happen to him who the first person they looking for? Me. when the police start asking questions around here the last thing people going say is they had some words last night in the club. Trip off this the whole room was quit, because I didn't make a sound or a move. The way he move next week he will have a problem with someone else.

Nosey looked at me and said that it sound good. I couldn't say nothing but laugh. Then I told everyone that tonight is all about Scrap my bother and my friend. So everyone please raise your glasses in honor of my love one Scrap I love you and may god walk with you.

CHAPTER FIFTEEN

The Truth

Five weeks passed it was a Friday morning nice outside. I had to handle some business. When I walked back into the bedroom Honey was sleep. She was looking so beautiful. So I left her sleep and went on to handle the bills and some other things. When I got to the garage I chose to drive Honeys car. I was in the street all day it was a cool day everything was hitting on point. Everyone I needed to see was on time. I talked to pimp Sue today and everything was going ok in Iowa. I talked to Everyday them in Detroit and its all well there too. It's around seven o'clock at night. I turned on the head lights on the car. As I was looking in my rearview mirror I saw a police make a u turn on Broadway and got right behind me. I wasn't tripping off the law because everything was right.

Right after I thought that he turned his lights on. I was like fuck! So I pulled over the first thing came to mind was to call Honey. So I did and she told me that one of her tail lights were out. I asked her why didn't she tell me that? She said you left me sleep this morning. Then I heard that knock on the glass. When I looked up the police man told me to give him my information. I pasted it to him through the window and he walked back towards his car.

I was setting in the car for about ten minutes. Then I saw another police car pull up in front of my car. I knew something was wrong. Then the first police walked back up to the car with his gun in his hand. Then he told me to get out of the car. Then he check me for guns and drugs. Then I was cuffed up and set on the ground. I asked him what have I done? He told me unpaid tickets. I told him that he had to be shiting me. As I set there I said to myself my day went from sugar to shit in a blink of an eye. Now I'm going to jail they towed my car. When we got to ST. LOUIS CITY head quarter it was around nine o'clock. I couldn't make a bond now I'm in here the whole weekend.

When I walked into the big holding cell I could tell it was going to be a long weekend. The cell was already packed. I had to take the steal bunk with no mat next to an old drunk. One thing I can say is he didn't smell. I also knew some of the guys that were up in here for the weekend. That was cool, that would give me someone to talk to. I tried to use the phone, but it was broke. So I laid down and went to sleep. That was a job itself, cause the old head next to me was making so much noise in his sleep. It took all night for me to fall off to sleep. When I did finally doze off it was lights out.

I felt someone touching me. then I heard a voice say youngster, hey youngster get up and eat. I got up and got my honey bun and coffee. I told the old head thank you for waking me up. He told me that it was nothing. Then I gave him half of my honey bun. He told me right on youngster, that was right on time. I have been here for a week already. I told him that was hard time. He told me that his bond was nine hundred dollars. Seems he didn't have it he had to do ninety days.

Then B.B and Sean came over and we started talking about the game. Who was doing it and ones that was just in the way. Time was flying by. Before I knew it, it was lunch time. When the food came, the old man was standing at the bars waiting. He called me to the front of the line and handed me the tray. After lunch b.b started in on about me being the man in the city. He said that my money was as long as train smoke. I started laughing. I told him that I was a poor man from Detroit. Then the old head said, you from Detroit youngster? I said, yeah. Then he said that there a lot of playas out of Detroit. Then sean said, what you know about being a playa, old man? He stood up and said, sit down youngster and let me teach you some things about the game. The game don't change, only the playa's do.

See I know a real Detroit playa. Even the police had respect for him. When he came to town I was selling fake at the bus station to the soldiers in the army from out of town. This particular game was called "the Jamaican drag". I can't and will not give it all to you. B.B said why not pops. Why? Have you heard the old saying that goes, the game is not to be told, it's to be sold. I couldn't do anything but smile. Now for those who don't know. The best playa's are those who have been played in the game before. I didn't get played this time on this particular game. How I learned this game was through an old playa from Detroit. Anyway school was now in session. He introduced us to a whole new world, and that world was the "Jamaican drag." He began to teach us how to form our words. So we could sound like we was from Jamaica. Trust me it was important for the game to work. So after about three weeks my friend smooth j had it down packed. He sound like he was from Kingston Jamaica.

Later on we learned that my friend from Detroit had a woman and a son living in St. Louis. So he was passing us some game out of respect of the game. So he told us that our grandfather was a surgeon. So naturally he had money. Anyway he died and left Antonio a lot of money. Sean asked him who was Antonio? The old man said it's smooth j youngster, listen! The only Antonio, which is smooth j, could get the money was that he had to get married. Now here he is in America, a Jamaican in need of help. The only person he knows is Mr. Raymond, his grandfathers attorney, and he's lost. Now this is when I come into play. Now I'm what you would call a cap man. In every game you have a cap man. My job was to steer and guide the mark. This is the most important thing of all. Long cons or short cons wouldn't be possible if people weren't trying to get something for nothing. Remember you can't beat a honest man. He's not trying to get or gain anything for nothing.

This was our very first lesson. I'll never forget it. It was a hot summer's day. It was three of us including my brother Paul, may he rest in peace. He was driving. The first rule of the game, never I mean never let the mark know where your car is parked. Smooth j and I had just left the car. We were parked on the side of veteran's hospital on Grand and Washington. While we was crossing the street, I could see a mark coming out of the check cashing place. E was smiling like a fat chess cat.

Now mind you smooth j and I had to separate until he was ready for me. He would rub his right elbow and I knew that was my "Que." When I saw that, I would walk towards them. He would asked me if I knew of a name of a place called the Radisson Hotel, at which I would say no. I would say that I've been living in St. Louis all my life and never heard of a hotel by that name. Now let me remind you that I'm the cap man. This is where I began. I would ask smooth j was there any other place than the Radisson hotel were he was trying to go. At that time smooth j would begin to tell me that he has been waiting on a cab driver. Who he had given a hundred dollars to, and that the cab driver told him to wait. So as the cap man, I asked him how long has he been waiting. He told me about a hour. Then I would tell him that the cab driver wasn't coming back. At this time I would ask him his name and where he was from?

At this time he would tell me that his name was Antonio and he was from Kingston Jamaica. He would go on to say that he was trying to go to the hotel, which meant any hotel. Remember I'm the cap man. It's my job to ask all the right questions. The mark is standing there listening to us talk. So, smooth j would tell the mark and I that he would give us fifty dollars a piece if we show him to a hotel. So I turn to the mark and ask him what he was doing, and if he had time to do this with me. of course I was adamant about it. So Antonio you are going to give us fifty dollars a piece, and we would look at the mark smiling. At the same time Antonio goes in his pocket and pulls out a mich. A mich is some cut up newspaper or monopoly money with a hundred or fifty dollar bill on top of it. That's when I tell Antonio not to flash his money like that. You are in St. Louis and you could get robbed. Now when I look at the mark, his eyes are as big as a Bo dollar.

Then I turn to Antonio and tell him that he needs to put his money in a safe place. Then that's when Antonio would tell us about his grandfather back at home, and how he didn't trust the white man in America. How the white man didn't give Americans their money back. That's when I would tell him where I bank and that I could show him. This is when you find out where the mark banks at. Then Antonio would say, my grandmother told me also that if you are a good man in America, they would give you a card that works. That's when I say identifications and pull out my I.D, and the mark pulls his out too. This way you get to see his or her address and their social security number.

That's some more game within itself. You could break into their home or get credit cards in their name. Then I pull out all my money and show it to Antonio. Then the mark does it right behind me. Sometimes they try to hold out, but it's my job to have them do so. Now I tell Antonio to let the mark bank his money. That's when I suggest that if he didn't trust us, that the two of us would put our money with his until we get to the bank. Of course Antonio was down with it. Then I take out my handkerchief, and the three of us put our money together. Did I tell you that the mark had sixteen hundred dollars from his income tax refund. I had a couple of hundred dollars. I didn't tell you that Antonio had a mich in his jock. That's nothing but newspaper in the shape of a bankroll in a handkercheif, now the mark has the mich. In the process of the three of us going to put the money in the bank Antonio gets leery and wants to personally hold the mich. Understand the mark has a problem with that, again it's my job to steer him. He naturally gives it up.

As we get closer to the bank, Antonio decides to give the Mich back to the mark. Then he tells the mark he feels comfortable and he trusts us. We changed the roll. We switched on his ass, but we never get to go to the bank. I asked, why? The police just so happen to be riding down Grand Ave. when they recognized the drag, they pulled over and asked us what we were doing at this time. They told us to get in, all three of us.

Once in the back seat, the soul brother on the passenger side turns all the way around. He asked Antonio what we were doing? At the same time smooth j broke the seal. What you mean by that is he started talking in plain English. You should have seen the way the mark was looking at him. I could read his mind. He was saying, mother fucker you are not from Jamaica. Smooth j told the police that the mark was lost and we were just showing him around. Then the police responded by saying," nigga if it wasn't so close for me to get off work, I would lock your ass under the dam jail."

He told me to walk one way. He told the mark to go another way. Smooth j had to walk another direction. When the mark got out of the car, he took off like a bat out of hell. He thought he had all the money. We fell out laughing. We took that paper to the playa from Detroit and we bought some tee's and blues from him. Shit I fucked up and started using them. Smooth j and play boy never looked back.

I asked him what ever happened to the guy from Detroit? He told me he was killed over some bullshit. Out of this shit we call the game the was a stand up guy. I miss him so much. He really had respect for the game.

We all laid back. I was in deep thought. I couldn't put my finger on it. I knew I had heard this voice before somewhere. Then they came with the food for dinner. After we were done, I had to ask him what was the name of the guy from Detroit? He asked why? I told him my people had been here since the eighty two. He looked at me and said, June. I just sat back on my bunk. Then I had to lie down and think. Then I asked him his name. He said Whoopsies. I told him my name was lil rose. He said lil rose, I have heard that name somewhere. Then I heard the turn key say lights out.

It was like two in the morning when I heard lil rose, lil rose get up playa. I rolled over and it was Whoopsies. I know where I heard your name from. I said where? He said June was your old man. Boy I haven't seen you in like fifteen years. How is your mother? I told him that she was doing okay. Then I asked him who was smooth J? He said you know who smooth j is. I said if I knew I wouldn't be asking. He said smooth j was jimmy. I asked him what ever happened to Jimmy? Well after your father died, I had to tell him. Don't you mean after my father was killed? Yeah lil rode, after your father was killed, jimmy ran the club and the business in the streets. He didn't have the knowledge or the vision like your father did to move towards the future. See lil rose your father had something none of us had. What was that? He had goals. To have a goal you must have what? I said the first thing to mind, "direction." He said right, because direction is the line or course along which a person or thing moves. I could remember sitting in my father's study, listening to him tell that same thing over and over again.

Whoopsies said goals. The only goals we wanted was on chains and rings. Then when he told us about direction, man we didn't know where we was going half of the time. He always said this at least ten times a day. Nothing I mean nothing is obtainable without discipline. We had none of what he called discipline.

Man jimmy ran the club into the ground. People loved June, but jimmy was a different story. People stop coming to the club, so that line of money dried up. Then he tried to do what he did best. That was to sale dope. Then he had some problems with slick. They had a war and slick shut jimmy down and almost killed him. Then I asked him was jimmy still alive? He looked at me and said, yes he is. I saw him a couple of months ago on the west side of town. Shit he is still getting high off that heron. I saw him over there by Page and Kings highway.

Whoopsies, I remember one day when I was younger. He was looking at me with a big smile on his face. I skipped school and was hiding in the basement of the club. He said, yeah that was your second home down there. I said yes it was, but this day jimmy called a meeting. A lot of people was there, but my father wasn't. this meeting here was not right. When my father had a meeting they were out in the open when the club was closed.

Whoopsies was still smiling. Then I said, but now as I listen to your voice, I can remember where I heard it at. The smile left his face as he said where? When the meeting was going on, jimmy put something on a piece of paper. When it got to you, you said man I'm not with this shit here! He told you to shut the fuck up before he put your name on the paper! Then he told all of you to read it and give it back to him so he could burn it. Whoopsies had a look of a thinking man on his face. I told him that was the day of my father's murder. He left with jimmy and never returned. That has been on my mind for years. I always felt I should have told my father about it. If I had, he might still be in my life. So my question to you is what was on that paper? We already know jimmy had something to do with the murder of my father. My people were the ones who tried to take him out at the playa's ball.

Whoopsies started by saying, he loved my father and he learned how to be a better man, just by knowing him. It was his name on that piece of paper. That night I was supposed to pick him up but I couldn't do it. That was the last time I saw jimmy for about ten years. When I left the club, I went out of town. I didn't have no parts of that snake shit. The way I saw it, you kill June, you kill me. The other guys involved was murdered the same night jimmy almost died. The last time I saw him, he was with his son. I said he got a son? What was his name? Lil jimmy, he is running the game off the west. I told him that this was a small world.

The next day was Sunday. They finally came to fix the phone. When I got my chance, I called Honey! When she answered the phone, she said rosewood? I said yeah. She started in on my ass. Where the fuck are you at? I told her that I was in jail. She said for what? I told her that it didn't matter, bond me out in the morning. I asked whoopsies his real name? when he told me I told Honey to pay his bill.

The next morning they called both of our names for a bunk and junk. Whoopsies told me thanks. I told him if he sees jimmy, don't tell him you know about me. he told me that he was going out of town when his money get right. I asked Honey how much money she had? She said she brought ten thousand and had eighty-five hundred left. I told her to give me seventy-five hundred, that would give us a thousand to get the car out of the impound. I gave whoopsies the seventy-five hundred and we took him to the bus station. I stayed there with him until he got on the bus. Honey left me there, she went to get the B.M.W out of the impounded, and towed it to the shop to get the tail light fixed.

CHAPTER SIXTEEN

The Beginning Of The End

When Honey came back to pick me up, I was just sitting out in front of the greyhound station. She had to blow the horn. When I got in she asked me what was wrong? I was just looking at her. Before I could say anything, she asked me who the old man was? I told her that he was an 0ld friend of my father. She then asked me what I give him that much money for? I said he gave me some important information.

When we arrived home, Honey ran me a hot bath. I had to roll me up some weed. I had to get my head right, as I sat in the tub. I asked Honey to fix me something to drink. When she came in the bathroom, she asked me again what was wrong? I told her that I discovered who killed my father and why? I wish you could have seen the look on my boo face. She looked at me and told me that she was sorry! After I got out the tub, I laid across the bed and told her everything that was said. What I learned from whoopsies, and what I heard in the basement all those years ago.

Then she asked the most important question. What are you going to do? For the first time I didn't know what to do. I knew one thing though. I had to kill jimmy. This wasn't business, this was personal. I got to be the one to pull the trigger on this one. Honey looked at me and told that she loves me, and take my time and be careful. I couldn't say anything. I just closed my eyes and went to sleep. A couple weeks passed. I had came up with something pretty sweet. Scrap was coming home from boot camp today. I was happy that I was going to see my peeps. We had rented a booth at the Broadway, a club on the eastside of town. The last couple of weeks

Honey and I weren't seeing eye to eye on shit. She has been spending a lot of time in the streets. I never seen her like this before. I went to the airport to pick up scrap. Today was kind of gray and wet. I must say I was proud of my little cousin. He chose to do something positive with his life. When I saw him in that uniform with his chest stuck out, I couldn't do nothing but smile.

Scrap walked up to me and said, hello rosewood. I said looking good play boy. He then told me that it was a place for you too! I told him that the street had me. So I told him that was a good thing for him. I also wanted to tell you that I'm proud of you for taking your own path in life. You are a man in my eyes. Fuck what anyone else say, you hear me? He shook his head, yeah cousin! I dropped him off at his mother's house, then I went to see my mother and brother. She was looking at me kind of funny. I asked her what was wrong. She told me to be careful today. I told her that I will. When I got in the car I was thinking about what my mother said. I was feeling on edge myself today. So when my mother said that to me, I had to take some time to get myself together. I went back to my house to put my vest on and grab my guns. I knew something was going down, I just couldn't put my finger on it. I came back to the hood to see how everything was going. I saw petty. We was on the porch talking when my phone rang. When I picked up, it was Pat. What's up play boy? Pat said it's not good up here. I asked, what's going on? He told me that Everyday, Sunny Boy, and Tarzan are locked up. I said what? Pat said, man check this out. Sunny Boy meet this cat. He was buying a quarter kilo every two to three weeks like clockwork. Last week he wanted to get two kilos, so Sunny Boy took him to meet Everyday. Everyday comes over to talk to me about checking this cats background. I said he took the cat to meet you? Pat said, no, just listen. So when everyday came over, Tarzan was over here. When Everyday got to talking about the cat, Tarzan said that he knew him. I asked him what was the word on the street? Well, Tarzan said that the dude was okay, he was just soft!

Pat say, man I fucked up. I asked how? I asked Everyday was he going to sale the cat the two kilos? Everyday said that he was. I asked when and where? He told me but Tarzan heard it. So when the drop went down, Tarzan and his crew came out of nowhere to rob the cat for the dope. Everyday sold the two birds to the cat. Then when the car started to pull off, Tarzan pulled right in front of the cats car in a truck. Then his crew pulled up behind the cat car in a truck. They jumped out with guns and jack the cat for the dope. I said okay. Pat said, then all hell broke out!

Come to find out, the cat was a c.i for the f.b.i. I said what? Pat said, yeah the f.b.i. they come from out of nowhere and locked Everyday and Tarzan asses up. I said but, and Pat cut me off. He said Sunny Boy was late to the drop. When he came everything was over. I told him about what happened. Then I asked did they lock the cat up? Pat said yeah, but you know the streets be watching.

The cat was on the street the next day like nothing happened. Sunny Boy caught right up to him. Sunny Boy killed that cat right in front of his girl and her mama. When I talked to him, he said he should have killed the girlfriend and her mother too! The police caught him at the bus station trying to board a bus. When they put him in a line up the at the police station, the girlfriend and her mother put a finger on him. So they got Sunny Boy on murder in the first degree, for premeditated murder of a federal informant. They got Tarzan crazy ass on robbery in the first degree, carjacking, unlawful use of a weapon, carrying a concealed weapon, and armed criminal action. Finally they got Everyday on drug trafficking, selling a control substance, and conspiracy to sale a control substance.

The only thing I could say was, damn! Then my phone went beep. I had call waiting so I told pat to hold on, I had another all. I clicked over, it was the investigator that I hired to follow Honey. His name was rock. I told him to hold on. I told pat that I had to hit him back on a later date, then I clicked back over to rock. Yeah rock, what's the word play boy? Rock started off by saying rosewood, it's not good. I have been watching her for the last two weeks. She have been hugged with a young man named little jimmy. I said what the fuck you mean she hugged up with a nigga named little jimmy? Rock said, one second. I cut him off and asked him did she go home with him. Rock said, yeah, jimmy jr. lives with jimmy sr. on academy on the Westside of town. The address is 911 academy. Do you have any pictures, I asked? He said, yeah! I'm on my way to pay you. I told petty that I would see him tonight at the club. He said okay, then I left to go meet rock. I saw scrap when I got ready to pull off he asked me what I was getting ready to do? I told him to get in, I'm on my way to the investigators office. I brought scrap up to speed. I asked him to do something important for me tonight. He said that he had my back. When I pulled up to rock's office, I told scrap to wait in the car for me! I went in, rock was a big white man sitting behind his desk. He stood up and shook my hand. Then he went right to the pictures. He showed me everything I needed to see.

Soon as I paid him, my beeper went off. When I saw the number, it was Honey. I used rocks phone to call her. I told her to meet me in the club tonight. She said okay then I hung up. I told rock thanks for everything. Then he gave me an address. I couldn't do nothing but smile.

When I made it back to the car, I was on a mission. I told scrap that I had to pick up a car I just put down on. I told him that he could keep my car tonight. He said that was cool. He could deal with that. I had scrap drop me off at the dealership. He saw my lac and told me that it was pretty. I told t him o meet me later at the club.

I rolled around for a couple of hours. No one knew about this new car, so I could move through the city free as a bird. I could go anywhere and I did. I went shopping at the mall. Then I got a room at the hotel. I took me a long bath and got dressed. I've been waiting for this night all my life.

I pulled up at the club around nine thirty. I parked on the back lot. I got out of my car with a big bag. When I got to the door, the bouncer asked me what was in the bag? I told him that it was a gift for the birthday boy. They checked it and I walked on in. the club was jumping. It seemed like the whole city was there. When I walked into v.i.p, I saw honey and little jimmy talking. I walked up to them. When honey saw me she tried to walk away from him. I grabbed her by the arm. I told her, hold up bitch. How are you? You have been with this nigga for the last couple of weeks." No I haven't!" I smacked the shit out of her before I knew it. Little jimmy pulled up on me. I told him the best thing for him to do was stay the fuck out of my business with his five dollar ass, before I make change!

I stepped to him, then the owner of the club pulled me to the side. Dave was a cool brother. He asked me what was up with me? I told him that I was fed up with that punk ass nigga little jimmy. Every time I step up in here we have problems. Dave said, Rosewood it's not you, last week jimmy had got into it with some other niggas.

I told Dave that I was gonna have him send jimmy and his crew some Champaign. Please tell him playa to playa. If honey has chosen him, I will respect the game and take my hat off to him. Dave said he could do that for me.

When I made it back to the V.i p room, I had to walk to the back. My booth was in the back corner between the bathroom on the right and an exit to the left. It was always a little darker in Vi.p. I had on some white cotton slacks, a white shirt, a blue vests, and some blue gaitors. I must say that I was clean.

When I made it to the table, I sat down with my crew. Honey was standing over at jimmy's booth. Dave walked over to jimmy's booth, he had a big bottle of bubbly with glasses. He ran the whole nine down to him. I was watching them from across the room. I lifted my glass to him, showing him the most respect from playa to playa! I got up and went to the restroom. A few seconds later scrap walked in and asked me was I cool. I said yeah, the question is are you cool? Scrap told me yeah, I told him let's do it.

When I walked out the restroom, honey was sitting at the table. She asked me did I do what I needed to do? I told her that it was over. She looked at me and said, Rosewood I love you! I told her, I love you too and thanks for all your help. She told me that I didn't have to thank her. I told her that I wanted her to always know how much I appreciated her. she started showing me her pretty smile.

I saw jimmy answer his phone. Then I saw him drop his head into his hands. The guys in his crew was asking him was he alright. then he started trashing the booth. He was yelling noooooooooooo, nooooooooo. Then he started crying. I heard later from Dave that little jimmy just found out that his father was killed at their house. I asked him who was he? Back in the day he had the city on lock. His name was big jimmy also known as smooth j. I told Dave that was fucked up.

Lets' go back a couple of hours, when he got the Champaign from me. That was for show. It was all for show. Do you remember when I said the streets was watching? Well she was, you wasn't though. When I went into the restroom and scrap came behind me. you didn't see the bag I brought in the club in his hands. See scrap is smaller than me. do you remember what I had on? Well I bought two of everything I had on, but a smaller size for scrap. We changed clothes. When we walked out of the restroom, Honey walked right up on him. Stood right in front of him, jimmy couldn't tell that it wasn't me. scrap and Honey was all hugged up with each other. you know how the make up thing go. It looked to everyone else that I was still there, but I changed in all black and slipped out the restroom window.

I went to the Westside of town, and knocked on jimmys back door. Rock had told me that they had a lot of traffic at the back door. The first thing that came to mind is that they were selling dope out of the back door. On Saturday, jimmy and his crew went to the club. This was my best opportunity to say hello to old uncle jimmy.

I parked in the alley and walked up to the back door. I took a deep breath and walked up to the back door. A man answered the door. He said hello. When he saw me he said what's up? I asked for jimmy. He said little jimmy was at the club. I said not little jimmy, but big jimmy. He asked me for what? I told him my name was lil rose. He said, lil rose, what's up lil nigga. I said what's up uncle jimmy. He said boy come into the light. Then I could see his eyes get big. He said, boy you look just like your father did. I said like he did when you killed him. He just looked at me. He said, boy what you talking about lil rose, you know better than anyone that I loved your father. I said, yeah you loved him to death.

I pulled my gun on him. He couldn't do nothing. He just looked at me like I was crazy. I told him to sit down on the steps. Then I asked him why? My father saw you as a brother! There wasn't anything he wouldn't do for you. Jimmy dropped his head in his hands and said in a low tone, I just wanted to be the man on top. As long as June was around, I would be second at everything. I got sick of people saying without June, there was no me. I thought he was weak, but I was wrong. I was the weak one of the two. I ran everything into the ground. I said, yes you did smooth j. he lifted his head up and said, whoopsies! I knew I should have killed him years ago. Then I heard the back gate close. I put my gun back behind my back. The lil guy walked up and asked jimmy if he had anything. Jimmy looked at me and said no, lil rose might have something. I told him play boy I don't get down like that. The little guy turned around and walked away. When I heard the gate close again, I put my gun back on him. I told him you killed my childhood when u killed my father, but my father never died! He lived through everyone else's memories that loved him. Except for you! You are a ghost. Soon as you leave a room you are forgotten!

He looked at me and said, fuck you bitch ass nigga! You don't have the heart. I put my gun to his forehead. Then I asked him, did he know what was mind blowing? He said what? Then I pulled the trigger. Bam!!!! His body fell back in the doorway. I reached in my pocket and pulled out some dope and threw it on him to make it look like a robbery. On my way back to the club, I beeped scrap. He walked back into the bathroom. He pulled me up and back through the window. I put my clothes back on and walked back to my booth. Scrap put his clothes back on and put the black clothes I had on in the drop ceiling. He walked out like nothing ever happened and we partied.

Then little jimmy got the all about his father passing away. I sent over some Champaign and told him that I've been there before, and how sorry I was. Then he left. A couple of weeks passed, the police said that it was drug related. No one saw me. Then little jimmy caught a break. Do you remember that smoker that walked up on me when I was at jimmy's that night? He told lil jimmy what he saw and heard. The only thing that stood out was the name lil rose. I was under investigation and didn't even know it.

Word on the street is that I killed lil jimmy's old man. There was a hundred thousand dollar target on my head. The street was on fire. I was on my way home about two in the morning. I was leaving one of my girlfriends house. I was standing at my car door trying to open it when I heard the shots ring out. Bam! Bam! Bam! Bam! Bam! Bam! Bam! Bam! Damn I was hit in the elbow. I saw a warehouse ahead.

I had to kick the door a couple of times before it finally crashed open. Shots rang out again. Bam! Bam! Bam! Bam! Bam! Bam! Bam! Bam! Bam! Bam! I had to jump through the doorway. There were bullet holes everywhere. Then I heard a cat say, what's up Rose mother fucking Wood? My job isn't done until I put two in your head. Then I said, at least let a playa die on his feet! Two of the cats pick me up and the third on put his gun to my forehead. I thought he pulled the trigger, I heard a bang! Then I saw flesh. I feel to the floor. My ears were ringing. I heard a couple of more shots, then, I heard the police. Freeze!

When I kicked the door in, it had an ADT alarm system. When I was hiding, I was really buying myself time. The police killed one of the cats, and the other two surrendered. While I was in the hospital, I was indicted by the feds for trafficking. I wasn't anything left for me to do, but shake my head and say, damn!

THE END

Made in the USA
Lexington, KY
29 July 2018